He didn't want her to have the job!

'Married nurses spend part of their working time worrying about their husbands and children, Professor,' Lucy said with icy politeness. 'Other nurses worry about their love-lives, and naturally I worry about my father sometimes, but he manages. If I thought he couldn't, then I wouldn't have returned to the Weston General.'

'And what about *your* love-life, Staff Nurse?' Joe went on smoothly, a little smile hovering about his mouth. I'm not discriminating against you because of your sex *or* your youth, but your marital state naturally concerns me.'

Why should it? she felt like flinging at him, it never mattered to you before!

Hazel Fisher was a late entrant into nursing and was briefly a general nursing student before deciding that psychiatry was her real interest. She worked as a mental nurse for several years before settling down to write full-time.

She has lived in East Sussex all her life, and now lives in a Downland village where she enjoys long walks with the dog, but admits that most of her nursing plots come to her when she's doing the household chores—particularly the ironing!

She enjoys reading and writing medical romances and says they provide a bit of much needed escapism— for her as well as for the readers!

Previous Titles

A DREAM WORTH SHARING
CALL AN ANGEL

LUCY'S CHALLENGE

BY

HAZEL FISHER

MILLS & BOON LIMITED
ETON HOUSE   18–24 PARADISE ROAD
RICHMOND   SURREY   TW9 1SR

First published in Great Britain 1991 by Mills & Boon Limited

© Hazel Fisher 1991

Australian copyright 1991 Philippine copyright 1991 This edition 1991

ISBN 0 263 77281 0

Set in 10 on 12 pt Linotron Times 03-9106-54332 Typeset in Great Britain by Centracet, Cambridge Made and printed in Great Britain

CHAPTER ONE

'The old man says he'll put my name forward for that course I was telling you about—"A Caring Doctor in the Community".' David Asher smiled across the canteen table at Staff Nurse Lucinda Powell, who started guiltily, hoping he wouldn't notice how far away she'd been.

'I'm glad for you,' Lucy said warmly, then pretended to notice the time. 'Heavens! I'll have to fly—the interview's at two-thirty.'

'I know—you've told me at least a dozen times this week. You must have gazed up at that clock a dozen times today, come to think of it!' David's smile was indulgent. 'I know the interview is more important than my problems, so rush off and get ready, there's a good girl.'

Lucy felt awful, realising how wrapped up she'd been in her own problems these past few weeks. David deserved better. Her eyes thanked him, then she sped away. It was a big step from staff nurse to sister, no matter how much experience a nurse had, and there was the 'old man's' opinion to contend with: the fastidious Mr Browne was retiring at the end of the year, but his opinion still carried weight. *And* there was Joe Kingsley.

Just thinking about Joe sent waves of apprehension through Lucy's body, or was it waves of desire? She wasn't sure any more. She only knew that her whole

world was about to come crashing down upon her—
Joe Kingsley was returning to the Weston General!

Once back in her room, she tried to concentrate on
the questions she might be asked at the interview. That
didn't help her nerves either, and she jumped when
there was a sharp tap at her door. Before she could
recover, the door burst open and her friend Heather
Baynes smiled down at her. 'Hello! You look awful,
Lucy,' she said candidly, settling herself at the foot of
the narrow bed, her eyes sympathetic.

'I *feel* awful, and thank you for telling me! I wish I'd
never applied for the wretched post,' Lucy admitted.
'If it were just an ordinary sister's post, I know I'd
stand a chance,' she went on firmly. 'But Arden is
special, and with this home-based experiment starting. . . And Mr Browne is such a stickler! If it were
anyone but him! It's because I left the hospital to work
as an agency nurse for a while. He regards it as
unethical, I think.'

'A rat leaving the sinking NHS ship to get more
money!' Heather laughed, peering into Lucy's mirror
and adjusting her cap.

'Agency nurses aren't *that* well paid, but you trying
telling him that!'

'The old man'll be retiring soon,' Heather coaxed.
'His successor might be quite different,' she went on in
a dreamy sort of voice, and Lucy opened her eyes
wide. Surely Joe wasn't here already?

'Heather——' Lucy paused, then began again. 'Have
you actually *met* his successor?' She held her breath,
waiting for the answer. Please don't say yes, she begged
silently.

'Mr Browne doesn't go until the end of the year—

right? But the new man is sitting in on the interview. He might start earlier, I suppose,' Heather added reflectively.

Lucy licked her suddenly dry lips. 'You'd better tell me what the new consultant is like.' She ran her fingers through her thick glossy brown hair, glad that she hadn't yet put it up for the interview. Heather's news had thrown her completely. Knowing that Joe Kingsley was coming back at the end of the year was bad enough, but to find that he was going to interview her. . .!

The window of her room overlooked the busy hospital campus, and she stared down at it, her blue eyes shadowed, barely listening to her friend's description of Joe Kingsley. Heather didn't know that she and Joe had met before, and Lucy wasn't about to enlighten her. 'Mr Browne can't fault my experience of life,' she said pensively. 'That's what they need on Arden, someone mature and experienced, but——'

'You haven't heard one word I've been saying!' Heather exclaimed. 'I was telling you he's got the most fabulous dark eyes, and all you can do is bleat on about Mr Browne!'

'Sorry! Nearly the witching hour, anyway,' she said brightly. 'Interview, here I come!' Then a thought struck her. 'Did you look in on Mrs Peterson? You were going to tell me how she was.' At Heather's stricken look, Lucy went on anxiously, 'She is all right, isn't she?'

'Don't be such a worrit, Lucy! I just forgot, that's all. We had a new admission and there wasn't time.'

'No, but you—I know, I'll look in on her after the interview. She'll want to hear about it, anyway. I promised,' Lucy went on firmly as Heather opened her mouth to protest. 'If you promise a patient something, you mustn't let her down.'

'No, Sister. Yes, of course, Sister!' Heather teased, and Lucy laughed, her problems forgotten for the moment.

'A quick transformation of the hair, then I'll be away.' Swiftly she twirled the thick hair up into a knot, watched admiringly by Heather.

'You're so quick and efficient, they won't be able to resist you, Lucy. Don't put yourself down. I know you've got an outsize inferiority complex but——'

'No, I haven't! Not really,' Lucy said quickly. 'It's just that this post means so much to me, and that's generally fatal. If you try too hard, you behave unnaturally. Just be yourself, that's what I tell students, but here I am ignoring my own advice! There, I'm neat and tidy now. Mr Browne and the new man shan't find fault with me—I won't let them.'

'That's it, Sister Powell. Show them what you're made of! Are you sure you'll recognise the new man? He's a real Latin type—dark of hair and bold of eye!' Heather giggled. 'He isn't a bad looker, either.'

'He's probably vain, then,' Lucy muttered, gathering up her cloak. Far better to go in mufti, but orders were orders. 'There. All ready—see you later!'

She rushed down the stairs in the nurses' home, glad that the interview was only in the next block, and she would have nearly ten minutes to settle down and look over the opposition before the interviews were even due to start. Leaving too much time wasn't a good idea, anyway—too much time to think, to dwell on the past.

By now walking at her usual brisk pace, she entered the spanking new block which housed most of the admin offices, and presented herself to the personnel officer's secretary.

'Staff Nurse Powell? Ah, yes—you're first!'

'Me? But I thought it was alphabetical order.'

'Yes, it is usually, but Professor Kingsley wanted to see the Weston General's staff first. Perfectly reasonable, I suppose,' the secretary added with a smile.

'Yes, perfectly,' Lucy agreed hollowly. The ordeal was nearer than she had thought!

There were five other nurses there already, only one of whom she knew, and she hurried across to her. Staff Nurse Robertson was fairly new to the hospital and Lucy didn't know her well, but at least she was Weston General too. She sank gratefully into a big squashy armchair. 'Hello, I'm Lucy Powell from Hathaway ward. Are you second for the interview?'

Hazel Robertson frowned. 'Yes, so I've been told. You're first, then?'

Lucy nodded, then turned to smile at the others, anxious to put them at their ease. Being interviewed at your own hospital by people you knew was bad enough, but it was ten times worse when everyone was a stranger. Lucy's sunny smile was just what the others needed, and the ice was soon broken.

One of the candidates was already a ward sister, with qualifications Lucy only dreamed about. Arden ward, where the new sister would be based, was the first link in the home-care chain. As Lucy understood it, the scheme was basically to rehabilitate patients and get them home as quickly as possible—far sooner than they might otherwise expect. Patients, mainly surgical, would be transferred from the main hospital, given a few days on Arden ward if necessary, then discharged home, thus leaving hospital beds for the more urgent cases. Once at home, they would be nursed for the first ten days or so by the special group of home-care nurses before being transferred to the usual district nursing team.

As Sister Shepham had a district nursing qualification, as well as rehabilitation ward experience, she seemed a certainty for the post. Well, as long as Mr Browne got a really experienced and *kind* sister, perhaps it didn't matter too much, Lucy told herself. There would be other posts for which she could apply.

Then her name was called and she struggled up from the comfortable armchair, knowing that she ought to have sat on a straight-backed chair as had Hazel Robertson, who was giving her a supercilious smile.

'Good luck, Nurse—Powley, did you say?'

With Nurse Robertson's tepid good wishes following her, Lucy took a deep breath, and knocked firmly at the door of the interview-room. Well, this was it, for better or worse! Bracing herself for the first glimpse of Joe Kingsley, she quietly went in and was welcomed by Mrs Morgan, the PNO.

'Staff Nurse Powell, do make yourself at home.' That was an impossibility, but now she was actually there Lucy's nerves vanished. Think of it as a practical assessment, she told herself. Forget Joe Kingsley.

Mr Ivor Browne, a thin, rather waspish figure, gave her a cold smile, which augured ill, but it was the tall lean man by his side who caught Lucy's attention, and she realised how stupid she had been—how *could* one forget Joe Kingsley?

'This is Staff Nurse Powell, sir,' Mrs Morgan was saying. 'Nurse Powell, Professor Kingsley, who will be taking over after Mr Browne retires.'

Automatically Lucy took the hand extended to her. 'Good afternoon, Professor,' she managed, then sank gratefully into the chair. When you'd had a shock, it was always best to sit down. It would have been nice to sit with her head between her knees, just to restore the oxygenated blood to her brain, but she would have to forgo that for now. Meanwhile, they were all staring at her, and she coloured fiercely. Had they asked her something and she hadn't heard them?

To her astonishment, it was Joe himself who explained away her apparent lack of attention. 'Staff Nurse and I have met before. I think she's rather surprised to see me. Isn't that right, Nurse?' Joe Kingsley turned on his charming smile, and Lucy nodded dumbly before she recovered her poise. Damn him!

Her thoughts must have been written on her face, for Joe smiled, probably enjoying her discomfort. His hard mouth softened a little, and those big dark eyes Heather had raved about weren't unfriendly.

Knowing she couldn't work with Joe again and that she had no chance anyway gave Lucy the impetus she needed, and she answered even the dour Mr Browne's questions with practised ease. It was only when he mentioned her time as an agency nurse that she tensed.

Mr Browne peered down at the notes in front of him, his steel-rimmed spectacles flashing their dislike of agency nurses. 'This agency, Nurse Powell—Call an Angel, or some such name,' he muttered.

'Call an Angel Nursing Agency, sir,' Lucy said

promptly. 'An angel for any emergency,' she added. 'I was there for nearly a year.' Carefully she avoided looking at Joe Kingsley, her attention on the older consultant.

'An angel for any emergency,' Mr Browne intoned, then exchanged a glance with Professor Kingsley. 'I've been in medicine long enough to know that nurses aren't angels,' he said drily, and Mrs Morgan chuckled.

Realising belatedly that it was a joke, Lucy forced herself to smile. 'It was good experience, Mr Browne,' she hurried on before he could launch his attack. 'I learned a lot about how patients cope at home. A patient's life doesn't begin and end in hospital,' she went on firmly, and Mr Browne looked astonished.

Before he could reprove her, Joe said smoothly, 'That's absolutely right, Nurse Powell. Just the sort of attitude we want for the new ward—isn't that so, Mrs Morgan?' Joe turned his devastating smile upon the PNO, who beamed.

'Quite right, Professor. Nurse has the right attitude.'

Well, that put a different complexion on things, and Lucy began to see that her fears had been groundless. Far from castigating her for leaving the hospital, Joe was applauding the fact—but then, he didn't know the real reason, did he?

'You look absurdly young, Staff Nurse.' That was Mr Browne, wading in again, but Lucy sensed that he'd given up his opposition to her. Joe's championing had done the trick.

Mindful of Sister Shepham waiting outside—the one with the extra qualifications—Lucy smiled serenely at Mr Browne. 'I can't help how young I look, sir, but it does cause problems sometimes,' she admitted candidly, and she sensed, rather than saw, Mrs Morgan's nod of approval. 'Patients don't always think I'm old enough to be fully trained, let alone in charge of a ward,' she went on, knowing she was refuelling Mr Browne's prejudices, but intending to demolish them as she went along. 'Relatives, in particular——'

'Ah, yes, the relatives!' The surgeon leaned forward. 'They need to be able to trust the sister of Arden ward, and would they feel they could trust you, I wonder?'

'They would soon learn that they could,' Lucy said firmly, well aware that his objections had some substance. She was nearly twenty-four, but could easily pass for twenty or less.

'There Nurse Powell rests on her laurels!' Joe Kingsley said lightly, and Mrs Morgan beamed again.

'And very substantial laurels they are, too! Nurse Powell is one of our most popular nurses—yes, with relatives, too, Mr Browne,' the PNO added, and to Lucy's astonishment the older surgeon's lips twitched as though he was going to laugh. 'If there are no more questions?' the PNO said, and Lucy relaxed. The ordeal was nearly over and she hadn't blotted her copybook too badly. Even the formidable Mr Browne was weakening.

But Joe hadn't finished with her, and she felt his eyes boring into her. Blue eyes met cold black ones, and they were cold now, as if he had been toying with her before and was now moving in for the kill.

'You seem well informed about the aims of Arden ward, but what about the home-care project as a whole? Initially the scheme will be funded by a charitable foundation, but what about afterwards—do you think we *need* a separate group of nurses?'

Lucy paused. It wasn't a question she had actually considered. 'The community nurses already have more work than they can cope with, so, yes, we need *more* nurses,' she said at last, 'but I don't know that they need to be a separate group. Surely, once the trial period is over, they could be integrated into the district nursing service, perhaps under the same manager?'

'A good point,' Joe commented, 'but what about the district nurses themselves? How do you think they might feel about our scheme for discharging patients early?'

Lucy already knew the answer to that. 'They aren't keen on the idea, sir. They feel that the home-care nurses will get all the interesting acute patients, and they will be left with the chronic sick and the old folks—all the heavy work,' she added, and Joe nodded.

'There's some truth in that,' he conceded, then, with an abrupt change of subject, he asked, 'Why did you become a agency nurse?' Joe's voice was calm and steady, so was his gaze, and Lucy did her best to answer honestly.

'My parents split up—after nearly twenty-six years,' she said, the memory still painful. 'My mother went back up north, and I stayed on at home to look after my father. Then he suffered a CVA—only a minor one,' she went on hastily, lest they think he needed full-time care. 'He manages all right alone now, and I live in the nurses' home, but at the time he needed me, and my agency duties fitted in better with my domestic commitments.'

Joe raised a dark brow, and Lucy's eyes followed the movement, much against her will. He wasn't a handsome man in the accepted sense of the word—his jaw was too strong, his mouth too wide—but he had charisma, and she genuinely liked looking at him, noticing something different every time she did so. The way his thick black hair wouldn't be tamed, the little smile that. . .

She swallowed nervously. Pull yourself together, Lucy! You haven't come here to admire Joe Kingsley; you've come to be interviewed for a job!

'And your mother—is she still living in the north? They haven't got back together again?'

'No, Mother remarried, actually,' Lucy said painfully. 'Then, last Christmas, her husband died. We don't see her at all now, but my father's content, I think. He's made a good recovery and neighbours pop in every day. I get home several times a week, and——'

'Ah! So half the time you're thinking about your father and his needs?' Joe suggested, and Lucy almost jumped up in her indignation, seeing where the innocent questioning had been leading. He didn't want her to have the job!

'Married nurses spend part of their working time worrying about their husbands and children, Professor,' she said with icy politeness. 'Other nurses worry about their love-lives, and naturally I worry about my father sometimes, but he manages. If I thought he couldn't, then I wouldn't have returned to the Weston General.'

'And what about *your* love-life, Staff Nurse?' Joe went on smoothly, a little smile hovering about his mouth. 'I'm not discriminating against you because of your sex *or* your youth, but your marital state naturally concerns me.'

Why should it? she felt like flinging at him. It never mattered to you before! 'I'm not engaged or going steady, if that was the question, Professor Kingsley,' she said placidly, giving him such an innocent smile that his eyes narrowed.

But he nodded as if satisfied, and as there weren't any more questions Lucy thankfully made her escape. Of course she wouldn't get the job now. Joe thought her mind would be elsewhere most of the time, but he couldn't be more wrong! In all fairness she couldn't blame him for the question, she supposed, but it was irksome nevertheless. Mrs Morgan might have mentioned David Asher, but that could hardly be counted as a romance, no matter what David himself might think.

After the interviews were completed, there was a tour of the soon-to-be-opened Arden ward. 'It will be a mixed ward, naturally,' the PNO was saying as they stopped briefly in the main ward area, where beds were already in place, in four-bedded cubicles. 'We shall have a large day-room where visitors will be welcome at any time. The support of relatives is an area which is all too often forgotten,' Mrs Morgan went on, 'but with funds from the foundation we intend to put that right. Now, through here——'

'Surely visitors will be confined to afternoons only?' Nurse Robertson queried. 'And evenings too, of course,' she hurried on into the sudden silence.

Lucy felt rather sorry for her, since the question didn't meet with Mrs Morgan's approval. 'That was suggested, certainly, and it would make carrying out the nursing procedures easier, but Professor Kingsley has decided that open visiting should mean just that.'

Mrs Morgan smiled at Joe, who gave Nurse Robertson a considering look which boded ill for her chances.

Afterwards they gathered in the PNO's sitting-room for coffee. The decision wouldn't be made for two or three days at least, and Lucy knew the coffee session and the tour of the wards were all part of the interview process.

Sitting quietly sipping her coffee and listening to Sister Shepham expounding one of her theories, Lucy wasn't at first aware that Joe was hovering by her side. She'd noticed that he had made a point of talking to each candidate informally and knew that sooner or later it would be her turn, but, even so, when he sat on the brocade-covered chair beside her she was unprepared and didn't know what to say to him. After all, what *could* you say to a man you had onced loved, a man to whom you had given your heart, only to have it flung back in your face? Warily she met his gaze, then heard that oh, so familiar chuckle.

'It's been a long time, little Lucy,' Joe said softly, his voice caressing her as it had so often in the past.

'Yes, so it has. About five years, isn't it? I'm not sure,' she went on, remembering very well. 'I was surprised to hear you were returning to the Weston. You went abroad, I know—is this your first post since then?' It was a struggle making polite conversation, but somehow she managed it, and felt rather proud of herself.

'Yes, I went abroad. To Saudi Arabia, then on to the States. I've an American doctor coming over shortly and she's looking forward to putting some of her ideas into practice,' Joe went on with a slight smile.

A female doctor—another conquest for the surgeon, perhaps? Lucy thought crossly.

Joe laughed softly. 'No, Lucy it isn't what you're thinking! I don't have designs on Dr Hamilton. She's quite a character; you'll like her. What have *you* been doing with yourself since we last met?'

'Nothing very exciting, I'm afraid,' Lucy murmured, realising as she said it that it was true. All the excitment had left her life when Joe Kingsley had. And now he was back, and all the old uncertainty had returned. She could feel his eyes on her, heating her even though they were in a room full of people. For, heaven help her, she still cared for Professor Joe Kingsley—the *married* Professor Joe Kingsley.

CHAPTER TWO

LIFE went on at the Weston General, and Lucy was thankful that she was run off her feet. The agony of suspense passed and she began to accept that she had been rejected. Joe Kingsley obviously didn't want her on his new ward, and Mr Browne's opposition could be taken for granted. Yet the challenge of the new-style nursing was exactly what she had wanted. She did want the post, she did!

Unaware that she had sighed, Lucy glanced up from the report she was writing—to meet the amused gaze of the man himself. 'Oh, good evening, Professor,' she murmured, making to rise, but a large, firm hand pushed her gently back again, his touch warming her through the thin white uniform.

Joe moved the visitor's chair slightly so that he could watch her, then held out a hand for the nursing magazine which lay on the desk. 'Is that this week's? There's an article about home-based care in it—did you read it?'

Pleased that she hadn't been caught out, Lucy handed him the magazine. 'Yes, I did. It sounds fascinating—but isn't there a lot of opposition to it?'

'Not as much as the media seem to think.' Joe's tone was frosty, and Lucy bent her head to the report again, unwilling to meet his gaze, but only too well aware that she was blushing. She ought to be past that kind of thing, and it irked her that his presence in the ward office could have that effect. Perhaps it was just as well she wasn't going to get the job!

'So—give me *your* opinion, Staff Nurse,' Joe said suddenly, closing the magazine and turning his brooding gaze upon her.

Lucy forced herself to concentrate, but it was an effort. 'I think it's an excellent idea, but I can see some of the problems,' she admitted, indicating the magazine. 'The health authority there was going to use agency nurses, and it's the private nursing aspect of it that upsets some people. You'll be employing only NHS nurses, won't you?'

'Yes, that's right. What we want is a specially funded team of nurses we can send out into the community to tend patients in their own homes—patients who would otherwise be taking up a hospital bed which might be desperately needed. We're going to run a six-month pilot scheme, and it's really intended for young or middle-aged people, those who are judged to be low dependency. Later we might take on a few terminal patients, but it's principally for the acutely ill.'

'You're having district-trained nurses only?'

'Mainly, yes,' Joe affirmed. 'They're the ones who would do the actual home nursing. But I also want a liaison nurse, someone who will get to know the patients to be given early discharge, then see them back home and into the care of our nurses, just for that important first week or so. In some hospitals there's been a breakdown in communications—people are discharged far too early and without any proper back-up. Sometimes even their GPs aren't told, and the patients end up being re-admitted. We don't want that happening here.'

Joe smiled his lazy smile, catching her unawares, and Lucy smiled back before she realised how unwise it was. The smile lit up her thin face, giving a sparkle to the limpid blue eyes, and this time it was Joe who glanced away, remembering that he mustn't get involved, not ever again.

He rose suddenly, his glance impersonal. 'Are there any problems before I go, Staff Nurse? Ivor's out at some fancy dinner and I promised I'd look in for him.'

That explained his presence, and Lucy began to relax. For a moment she had thought he had come to tell her she'd been turned down, but of course an important man like that wouldn't bother.

'No, there's nothing in particular worrying me, thank you, sir. Unless you wanted to see Mrs Holme? Sister says she should be first for early discharge, but——'

'But the home facilities are inadequate, so we'll have to keep her longer,' Joe finished, and Lucy gave a wry smile.

'That's something we're going to find often. It's that sort of neighbourhood, isn't it?'

'Problems, problems, everywhere we look. Don't take it to heart—you worry too much, little Lucy.'

Lucy turned her startled gaze to him, to catch a fleeting glimpse of what might have been genuine affection. But his expression hardened even as she watched, and she knew she must have been mistaken.

Joe had never loved her, she thought, watching his tall figure striding away, her eyes still lingering on the swing doors even after he was out of sight. A summer affair, that was all it had been—yet he had spoken words of love, words which were still engraved upon her heart. That was what hurt so much; that he had been deceitful, utterly without principle—leaving her to find out afterwards that there was a Mrs Joe Kingsley.

Bitterly Lucy shut him out of her thoughts, and bent her head once more to the report. But the words danced in front of her, and she got up to do yet another round of the ward, even though she had been in there only twenty minutes before. Work, work and yet more work—that was the cure, wasn't it?

Another long day had passed without word from the powers that be, and Lucy knew they would contact the lucky one first, then tell the others. Still, it wasn't the end of the world, as David was always telling her— *David*!

Heavens, she'd forgotten David! She almost ran up the stairs of the nurses home, had a wash then grabbed the first outfit to hand—a vivid cerise shirt and black skirt. That would do nicely. David never commented on what she wore, not like Joe. . .

But then he would, wouldn't he? Part of the married man's practised charm. Swallowing the tears that sprang unbidden to her eyes, Lucy walked slowly down the stairs, forgetting that she was already late for her date, and that David would be cooling his heels in the doctors' common-room.

David wasn't there, and she was told that he was probably still on the ward. 'The new man, Professor Kingsley—David's walking the wards with him,' one junior doctor offered, and a puzzled Lucy wondered what to do next. She could hardly go looking for him, so decided to compromise by waiting in the nurses' sitting-room.

The room was empty, the television blasting forth to an invisible audience, and Lucy quickly switched it off. She needed to think, yet too much thought was a bad thing, for whenever she closed her eyes and tried to relax it was the dark eyes of Joe Kingsley she saw quite clearly, not the light blue ones of David Asher.

Why had Joe returned? It didn't make sense. The Weston General wasn't a teaching hospital, even though it was the biggest hospital in the Warwickshire area. He might easily have gravitated towards the big London hospitals, or even one in his native Tyneside.

It was funny to think that Mum and Joe both came from the same region. Lucy's lips curved into a smile as she remembered Joe once teaching her some Geordie words—then being surprised because she knew them already. There was one word she hadn't known, though—Joe had called her his little 'flower'. Ridiculous. Of all the words to bring tears to her eyes, it was that one, and hastily she opened her eyes, reaching for a tissue.

'Ah! Thought you'd be here!' A tall man was smiling down at her, and just for one wonderful moment Lucy believed it was Joe Kingsley. 'Sorry I'm late,' David went on, flopping down on the chair next to her. 'My new "old man" decided to do a surprise round and I got caught up.'

Lucy swallowed the lump in her throat, her eyes still bright with unshed tears. Carefully averting her face, she managed a laugh, and David didn't appear to notice anything amiss. 'Trust you! Anyway, I'll bet you volunteered! How is he—compared with Mr Browne, I mean?'

It hurt, talking about him like this, yet it gave her a

vicarious pleasure, too, and David could always be relied upon to discuss his consultants and their foibles.

He shrugged, then moved uneasily. 'He's all right, I guess. I prefer old Ivor, though. Anyway, are you ready?'

A disappointed Lucy got up, thinking it odd that David didn't want to discuss Joe, but perhaps he would once they developed a sound working relationship. That was the only relationship *she* intended to develop with the new man, anyway!

'Damn nuisance, old Kingsley turning up like that,' David grumbled, once he'd set his old Escort in motion. 'I wanted to get away and——'

'He isn't old!' Lucy exclaimed before she could help herself. 'He can't be more than forty, can he?' Joe was thirty-seven but she wasn't about to tell David.

'He isn't young,' David said testily, then had to brake hard as someone jaywalked across the road leading to Leamington. 'Damn fool! He deserves to end up in Casualty!' he snapped.

'If you're in a bad mood, perhaps I'd better get out and walk!' Lucy was cross now. All of a sudden she didn't want to spend the evening with David's talkative sister. She wanted to be alone, stupid though that might be.

'Don't be silly, darling.' David's good humour was restored instantly, and Lucy felt mean. 'There's so much I wanted to say this evening, and I haven't had a chance, thanks to old Kingsley,' David said as they drew near his sister's house. Switching off the engine, he turned to Lucy.

'Haven't run out of petrol, have you?' she said lightly. 'Or have you heard about the job and you're afraid to tell me I haven't got it? I know that, anyway,' she hurried on, trying to smile.

'Oh, Lucy, love!' David's arms closed about her, and she rested her head thankfully on his shoulder. If only she could tell him about Joe! If only. . . But some things were better left unsaid. David wouldn't understand, and that saddened her. The man she almost loved—well, was *fond* of, anyway—and she couldn't unburden herself to him.

'It's all right, David, really.' Lucy struggled against his arms but he wouldn't let go.

'No, it isn't all right! I'm asking you to marry me— well, later on, when I get to be senior registrar—and I feel for you, not getting the job. But I can't say I'm sorry. Old Geordie Joe would have you running about here, there and everywhere! The man's a slave-driver! I'd never see you,' David complained, and this time Lucy *did* struggle free.

'Is he a Geordie? He hasn't got the accent. Not like my mother,' Lucy hurried on, for something to say.

'Don't change the subject, Lucy. Will you marry me, my dearest heart? There, how's that for a romantic proposal!' David laughed, but Lucy could feel the uncertainty emanating from him in waves.

'David——' she turned to him, spreading her hands helplessly '—I don't *want* to get married. Not yet, anyway. I want to be a ward sister—I *like* nursing. It's my career, just as surgery is yours, and I don't think I'd want to do just part-time.'

'You could take the Pill, couldn't you? It isn't as if we'd want a family straight away,' David pointed out. 'I can't *afford* a family, anyway.'

Lucy's heart twisted in her, and she snuggled up to

David, putting her arms around him, her turn to offer comfort. 'It's not that I want a lot of children. . .' she began again, and David chuckled.

'I'm glad about that!'

'Eventually I want to settle down and marry, have three children and a dear little house with roses around the door and a sundial, and——'

'And a nice piece of lawn at the back for me to mow when I come home from my twelve-hour day!'

'Yes, something like that,' Lucy agreed solemnly. 'Somewhere warm and sunny and——' She broke off, remembering Joe's description of his cottage up north. Wild and wonderful, lonely, a haven to return to after a hard day's surgery. Cold, with winds sweeping in straight from Siberia, but warm and cosy inside. He had turned to her then, holding out his arms. Warm and snug in his embrace, Lucy had felt that any amount of cold winds from Siberia wouldn't have bothered her.

'Lucy, what is it, love? You've gone pale.' David began rubbing her hands, talking to her gently, and gradually she returned to Warwickshire, Siberia and the cold northlands an elusive and imaginary memory, for she had never seen Joe's cottage.

She shook herself. 'It's nothing; I think I'm getting a cold. And I'm awfully hungry!'

'No sooner said than done!' Hurriedly Dàvid started up again, and a dazed Lucy settled back in the seat, her mind conjuring up a landscape she had never seen.

It was lunchtime the following day that the official-looking letter was left in her pigeon-hole at the hospital, and the hall porter handed it to her with a smile that Lucy found difficult to return.

Since she was on duty she couldn't stop to read it, but then she didn't need to. Wondering who had got the position, she hurried to her ward, arriving just as Joe Kingsley and Mr Browne were leaving.

Of course! It was a ward-round morning, and she'd clean forgotten. Other events had pushed that important fact to the back of her mind, and she stood aside to let the consultants and their entourage pass. Mr Browne looked right through her, but then he always did. Joe paused, though, and Lucy fixed a bright smile to her face. She would not let him see how disappointed she was. She had her pride, and that was about all she had left now.

'Might I have a word, Staff Nurse?' Joe raised an eyebrow at her hesitation, and Lucy could feel herself going pink.

'Oh, yes, of course, sir. Where——?'

'In the treatment room will do nicely. It should be free now.' Joe indicated that she should precede him, and, wonderingly, she did so, and was surprised and dismayed when he carefully closed the door behind them.

Nervously she waited for Joe's words of condolence, though why he should bother, she didn't know. It was a nice gesture on his part, anyway, and the smile she summoned up this time held real warmth.

'I take it you've had a letter this morning? About the ward sister's position?' he began, and Lucy nodded.

'Yes, but I haven't had time to read it yet. I knew I'd been rejected, though.'

Joe frowned. 'Do you always expect rejection, Staff Nurse? I like positive thinking from my nurses.'

'I'm sorry about that, Professor, but there was a far

better qualified candidate at the interview and I assumed she would be given the position. I would have given it to her, anyway,' she admitted, and Joe chuckled.

It hurt watching him, seeing the way the lines vanished from his nose and mouth, the way those sensuous lips parted to reveal perfect white teeth, the way his eyes warmed, laughing at her. . .

'If you mean Sister Shepham, then yes, she *did* get the post,' Joe admitted.

'I'm pleased for her. There'll be other jobs I can apply for.' At least she knew now, and it *was* kind of Joe to tell her in person. 'Thank you for letting me know. I was wondering who had been given the job. I liked Sister Shepham.'

'So did I. So, naturally, did Ivor. She was favourite from the moment she came through the door,' Joe said with a wry smile, and Lucy looked her surprise. 'She's past thirty and not particularly attractive, and Ivor approved of that. She won't be leaving to get pregnant in a couple of years, "Not like the pretty young one", he said! He meant you, I believe,' Joe added meaningly, and she flushed.

'He's wrong there. I shan't be getting pregnant—*or* married yet awhile. Anyway, it's possible to marry and still keep on with a career.'

'Yes, I agree, but he doesn't see it that way,' Joe said easily.

'Well, thank you again. It was kind of you to——' Lucy began, but Joe brushed her words aside.

'I haven't made a point of telling you something you can read in that letter! I have other things to do,' he pointed out coldly, and the Joe she'd known vanished as if he had never been.

'Then why bother to tell me?' she demanded. 'You've shut us in here and you know what the hospital grapevine is like,' she went on testily. Hadn't it told her about Joe's wife? On that occasion it had spoken the truth, but this time it might get it wrong, and it would be all over the hospital that Staff Nurse Powell was having an affair with Professor Kingsley!

'Now just *what* might the grapevine say about us, Nurse?' Joe folded his arms and leaned back against the door, looking so handsome and desirable that Lucy had to look away.

'You surely don't need me to tell you!' she said crisply. 'What *did* you want?'

'I wondered when you would ask, little Lucy,' he said softly, and she flinched as if she'd been struck.

'Please don't keep calling me that. I'm not little Lucy any more. I'm a trained nurse—not a nineteen-year-old student nurse with stars in her eyes!' she flung at him.

The temperature dropped several degrees in a room that was always cool, anyway, but she didn't wish the words unsaid. It was about time he realised how much she had been hurt. By calling her 'little Lucy' it might seem that he wanted another affair with her—well, he was out of luck this time!

Joe smiled grimly, watching the varied expressions chasing themselves across Lucy's face. If only she didn't look so vulnerable, so easily hurt, so utterly adorable. . . 'You remember my telling you about the liaison nurse I wanted to help set up the home-care scheme?'

'Yes, I remember. Will Sister Shepham be doing

that, as well?' It was a stupid question, Lucy knew; the woman couldn't be expected to do both. Then a thought struck her and her eyes widened, just the faintest hope dawning in them.

'Yes, that's what I want *you* for, Staff Nurse Powell,' Joe said formally, and Lucy opened her mouth in astonishment but no words came out.

'Close your mouth—it's tempting me. Mrs Morgan will fill you in on the details—I just wanted to give you the good news first. I'm glad I did,' Joe finished, and now it was his turn to glance away. He had spoken the truth; she *was* tempting him, just by being Lucy. Giving her the job was a mistake but it was too late now to change his mind. 'The best of luck,' he added, then strode out, closing the door behind him, leaving a shaken Lucy to gaze wonderingly into space.

She was to be Joe's liaison nurse! She and Joe would be working together, after all—with all the dangers that entailed.

'The great day on Monday, then!' Heather rushed up to Lucy, who was walking Hathaway ward as a staff nurse for the last time. 'We shan't know you in your glamorous designer clothes!' Are you really not having to wear uniform?'

'Well—the chief says I needn't if I don't want to. He would prefer me to wear either a plain suit or just the uniform dress without a cap,' Lucy confided. 'I'm certainly going to wear high heels, though! It's all right for you—you're tall!'

Heather wrinkled her nose. 'Being tiny has its advantages—the five-feet-two types make strong men weak at the knees! Anyway, I shall miss you. So will the patients.'

'I'm not going hundreds of miles away, Heather! I'll still be spending part of the time on the ward, but not doing actual nursing. I'll miss that—I hadn't thought until now, but I won't be doing *any* nursing, will I? Anyway, I must get on—I'm still supposed to be ward-nursing today.' She hurried away, heading straight for her favourite patient—the oldest woman in the ward, Mrs Fleming. 'I've come to give you a little wash and make you nice and comfortable,' she murmured, patting the old lady's cheek gently.

Mrs Fleming snorted. 'If you really cared about us you wouldn't be leaving the ward! Going off to do some fancy private nursing!' she went on, and Lucy raised a brow.

'Am I? No one told me,' she said, swiftly drawing the bed curtains. 'I'm going to be a sort of rehabilitation nurse, working with Professor Kingsley. He's your surgeon, the one with the nice dark eyes. That's hardly being a private nurse, is it?'

Even as she spoke, Lucy began easing the portly woman up in bed. 'The student nurse will be along in a minute to help me, but I can make a start anyway. We're pretty busy today, being an ops day.'

'That nurse what come on relief—*she* said you was going to private nursing. Professor Kingsley's private nurse, she called you,' Mrs Fleming said stubbornly, and Lucy stopped for a moment, her eyes dark with pain.

If only she *could* be Professor Kingsley's private nurse! 'If you mean Staff Nurse Robertson, she should know better. I'm a sort of halfway nurse, really!' she smiled, and Mrs Fleming cackled.

Professor Kingsley's private nurse. Lucy hoped Hazel Robertson wasn't going around saying that to patients. It sounded awful and gave quite the wrong impression. True, she wasn't sure exactly what her duties would be, but all would be revealed three days from now when she began working with Joe.

The student arrived then, and Lucy resolutely put Joe Kingsley from her mind. Being Joe's liaison nurse would probably be bad for her blood-pressure, but time would tell.

She was spending her days off at home, but she was later leaving than she had intended, and the car park was almost empty as she left the main building. There had been a small memento from the staff of Hathaway ward, something Lucy hadn't expected. For a moment she had been afraid they were going to adhere to tradition and give her the cold bath reserved for trained nurses who left! Instead, the girls had bought her a pretty cosmetic bag and a set of cosmetic brushes.

Still smiling at the thought, Lucy was about to unlock the door of her Mini when she heard footsteps, and a tall figure came striding towards her. For one moment. . . Then she realised that her eyes weren't deceiving her—it *was* Joe Kingsley.

'Still here, Staff Nurse?'

Lucy's tired mind couldn't really take in the fact that Joe was beside her. 'Oh! Yes, I'm still here!' Her voice was unsteady. 'I'm going home for my days off,' she rushed on, then tried to stifle a yawn. If there had been a bed under her right then she would have dropped off to sleep in an instant.

'It's been quite a day for you, hasn't it?' Joe said easily. 'You've had all the trauma of leaving your old ward and the worry of tackling something completely new.'

She tensed, wishing suddenly that they weren't alone. Joe must have shaved recently and he smelled clean and fresh, the tangy aftershave bringing back memories she wished had stayed buried. 'Yes, I——' She stopped, his nearness unnerving her. Here they were, alone in the huge car park, and she could think of nothing to say! 'I'll miss Hathaway ward,' she managed at last. 'I've been happy there.'

'I hope you'll be happy in the new unit,' Joe said softly, his voice caressing her. Then reality returned. 'I must get back to my own hearth,' he added, and Lucy forced a smile.

Back to his own hearth—back to his wife? 'Yes, of course, sir. I'll see you on Monday.'

'Monday—eight o'clock sharp. Goodnight, little Lucy. Drive carefully.' Lucy felt the brief pressure of his hand on hers, then he was striding away to the senior staff car park. Lucy watched him, her thoughts in turmoil, the words she ought to have spoken tumbling over one another in their eagerness to get out.

What a fool he must think her! Wearily she set off, trying unsuccessfully to push Joe Kingsley to the back of her mind—the man she had once loved; the man she *still* loved.

Her father was delighted to see her, but his eyes were anxious as they searched her face. 'Lucy, love, what's the matter?'

'I'm fine, Dad, really,' Lucy hastened to reassure

him, 'just bone-tired, that's all. I shall fall into bed, I warn you!'

'Your mother phoned and we had a long chat,' Dad was saying, and Lucy managed to nod and give the appearance of being interested. And of course she *was*, but right now all she wanted was her bed—bed, and a long dreamless sleep, but somehow she felt her sleep wouldn't be dreamless. Oh, Joe! her heart cried, I still love you! And I mustn't, I mustn't!

'She wants to come back to see us both,' her father went on, and Lucy murmured an appropriate response.

'Do you think she might come back to me?' he went on hopefully, turning up the gas under the kettle.

'Come back? Dad, she can't! She won't, not now,' Lucy amended.

'But she might!' Her father's hands were trembling so much that the mug in his hand rattled against its saucer. He went on stubbornly, 'We were together a long time—divorce can't alter that.'

Divorce couldn't alter the fact that her parents' married life had been one long quarrel, Lucy thought, but remained silent.

'His—her husband's daughter, *she's* been a grand help, apparently,' he said brokenly. 'Nice of her, wasn't it? Mum said she didn't know how she would have coped without her. Of course, she really wanted you but——'

'But nothing of the sort!' Lucy was hurt, but not surprised. 'You know I've always been Daddy's girl!' Fondly she dropped a kiss on her father's brow, then took the mug from him. 'You'll drop this if I don't take charge! I'd like to meet the daughter, though,' she added, realising that it was true. To have a stepsister and not know her! 'Perhaps if Mum comes down she'll bring Sadie with her. I've always wanted a sister. Well, a brother, really,' she teased. 'Two men in the family for me to boss about!'

'And you were a little bossy boots when you were a youngster, and no mistake!' Her father had perked up all of a sudden. 'I'll have a cup with you. It's nice being waited on again!'

And you would like me back permanently, Lucy thought. 'While I'm working for Professor Kingsley I could live at home again, if you would like that, Dad?' she offered later.

His face lit up for an instant, then he waved away the suggestion. 'No, don't you worry. If your Mum's coming back, even for a few days, I'll have company enough. Will you mind if she does bring Sadie down with her?'

'No! I told you, I'd be delighted. I can show her a few of the sights. Now—off to bed with you,' Lucy ordered firmly, and smiled to herself as her father meekly obeyed. He still had a limp, but it was barely noticeable now, and he had almost recovered the use of his left arm. He'd slowed up, though. He wasn't the man he had been even five years before, and she wondered whether her mother realised that. Poor Mum.

But poor Mum doesn't need me, Lucy thought sadly as she undressed in the room that had once been hers. No one needs me, not even Joe. . .

Lucy's days off passed in a flash, and before she knew it it was Monday and she was just approaching the Weston General.

A new day, a new week, and a new job. What more could she want? She let her shoulders droop just a little, the happy smile she had kept pinned to her face for her father's sake fading as well. Today she would be working for Professor Joe Kingsley, an important surgeon, a man to look up to and respect, and she'd better not forget that. The fact that he was also the man she had once loved and lost mattered not a jot.

Lucy wandered into the echoing building. The night staff were still hard at work, the admin people wouldn't be around for another hour at least, and it gave her a pleasant feeling of oneness with the hospital. She had liked night duty, and when this job ended she might just go back to that. A spell on night duty would ease——

'Early bird, Lucy, love!' David fell into step beside her, smiling down at her.

Lucy returned the smile. 'You're looking remarkably bright and cheerful for so early in the morning! You haven't been up all night, have you?'

'No, it's the new schedules the Prof worked out. I've found I'm getting more time off, not less,' David confessed, then bent and planted a kiss on her cheek. 'Mmm, I've missed you, love. Been busy at home, have you?'

'So you're friends with the Professor now?' Lucy said lightly. 'And yes, I *have* been busy at home—getting my father's washing up to date and mowing the lawns!'

'Well, he's all right, I suppose—the Prof, I mean,' David admitted. 'I went on about him a bit, didn't I? It was just his high-handed manner and——'

'He hasn't got a high-handed manner! Has he?' Lucy

went on hastily, and thought David gave her a strange look, though he said nothing.

'Looking forward to your new job, are you?' he said instead. 'I must say, you look very cool and professional. High heels suit you. He might not approve, though,' David warned, and Lucy shrugged.

'I doubt that he'll notice. Anyway, have a good day!' They stopped outside the door of Arden ward, where she was to be based initially.

'How about lunch? I'm off at twelve-thirty today, with a bit of luck—OK?'

Lucy hesitated. 'I'd love to, but I'm not sure of my hours. I haven't got regular shifts to work now, you know. I don't know quite *what* hours I'll be working,' she admitted, and David frowned.

'I told you he was high-handed and you nearly bit my head off, Lucy. He *is*, so be warned—though of course you knew him before, didn't you?' he went on quickly, his anxious eyes searching her face, and Lucy flushed.

'Well, yes, yes, I did, but that was a long time ago, before I left to join the agency and——'

'Why didn't you tell me?' he demanded. 'I was left to find out from the Weston General grapevine! It's too much, Lucy, it really is! I thought we had an arrangement!'

'An arrangement? About what?' Oh, look, there's Sister Shepham! Two new girls together—see you!' Glad of the chance to escape, Lucy pushed her way through the swing doors of the ward. What arrangement was she supposed to have with David? He might think he loved her enough to marry her, but she knew otherwise. No, she was footloose and fancy-free, and always would be. David couldn't take Joe's place in her heart; no one could. If she couldn't have Joe she wanted no man.

To her consternation, the man himself was already on the ward. But she needn't have worried: his smile was cool, professional, his manner no more than friendly as he welcomed her.

'Two early birds! That's good; I've a lot to get through today. Now, here's your schedule for the week.' Joe handed her a typed sheet of paper. 'My secretary's a treasure, but I doubt if she's left you enough time for all your visits. Check back with Sister Shepham if things aren't to your liking.'

Lucy and the new sister exchanged rueful smiles. 'What I would like to know is where are all the patients I was promised?' Sister Shepham asked briskly, and Joe chuckled.

Lucy pretended not to notice, and began diligently reading her schedule. As far as she could see, most of her time would be spent just talking to patients this first week, both in the ward and at home. Then there would be the liaison with the social services, district nurses, meals-on-wheels and so on. As Joe had said, it was important that, if patients were sent home early, everything was ready for them. They mustn't suffer because of some administrative failure, as had happened in London some time ago when several patients were discharged to totally inadequate homes, and with no proper nursing or medical back-up.

'You'll be kept pretty busy, Nurse Powell,' Joe warned, and Lucy glanced up, her eyes dancing.

'Yes, I think you're right! Do you want me to help Sister this morning? It's too early for——'

'Good idea. Make yourself useful generally,' Joe cut in, then the telephone pealed and he was the nearest to it. 'Good morning, Arden ward. Oh, it's you, Rosemary.'

Joe's tone had cooled but Sister Shepham appeared to notice nothing. 'Call me Edna, and you're Lucy, aren't you? Fine. Now what I'd like first is——'

Lucy heard the woman's voice and she supposed she must have made some response, but, try as she might, she couldn't concentrate. Her eyes were on the tall lean man speaking on the telephone. He appeared angry, but then Rosemary always made him angry. Lucy knew that now—she also knew that Rosemary was Mrs Joe Kingsley.

CHAPTER THREE

'I'M OVER the moon about going home tomorrow, Nurse—is it really true?' Eighty-eight-year-old Annie Pierson clutched at Lucy's hand, her eyes begging to be told the truth.

'Yes, it's really true—Professor Kingsley wouldn't lie to you, Mrs Pierson. We've laid on all the nursing services, and meals-on-wheels, home help. . .' Lucy ticked each item off on her fingers. 'You'll be looked after twenty-four hours a day, just until you get on your feet again.'

Mrs Pierson was spending her last day as a patient at the Weston. Her hip-replacement operation had gone satisfactorily, though privately Lucy thought the woman too old and frail to be turned out of hospital, no matter *how* many district nurses there were to look after her. But at least she would be given every care, and the team would carry on with the rehabilitation begun on Arden.

After telling the sister that she was leaving the ward, Lucy went in search of Heather. In the two weeks she had been working for Joe Kingsley, she'd seen hardly anything of Heather, and it worried her. They had been such great friends before. David was right about Joe's being a hard taskmaster—every time she thought she had finished for the day, he came up with some other little chore. Of course, she didn't mind, but it meant she saw little of David as well as Heather. And, unfortunately, she saw far too much of Professor Joe Kingsley.

It was as if he was deliberately seeking her out, Lucy mused as her steps took her past his office. Frowning, she turned back, never having intended coming as far along the corridor as this.

'Ah, Staff Nurse Powell,' a deep voice hailed her, and she stopped again. Of course, she'd had no idea he was in, and it was pure chance her steps had brought her this way, but. . .

'You wanted me, Professor?' she asked politely, then blushed as she realised what she'd said.

Joe's smile was crooked. Yes, he wanted her very much indeed, and his carefully arranged plan to get her out of his system wasn't working at all—far from it. 'How did you find Mrs Pierson?'

Lucy smiled brightly and proceeded to tell him about the patient. 'She only half believed me when I con- firmed that she would be going home tomorrow,' she finished. 'She thinks it's too good to be true! She told me she thought she'd come into hospital to die,' she added, her eyes sad, and Joe had the almost irresistible urge to draw her into the comfort of his arms, kiss away that sad expression. . .

'She *is* going to die, Staff,' he said instead. 'That's why I want her home. I guess you thought she wasn't suitable for home care?' he went on, and, surprised, Lucy nodded.

She hesitated. 'You asked me about my agency experience with terminal patients—is this something you intend doing in the future? I mean, branching out——'

'Yes, that's right,' Joe cut in, 'but I can't stop now—

look, why don't you join me for dinner one evening? Bring a list of your questions, and we'll discuss them over a meal—if you can spare the time?'

If she could spare the time? Trying to hide her pleasure at the unexpected invitation was difficult, but Lucy managed it somehow, and was rather proud of her cool, controlled smile as she accepted. Of course, David wouldn't like it, but once she'd explained that it was purely business he would understand, surely?

Unfortunately David didn't understand, and the look he gave her was part-incredulous, part-scornful. 'Sucking up to the new man won't get you very far, Lucy—he's hewn out of granite! He's a typical northerner,' he went on bitterly, and Lucy gasped.

'Apart from the fact that *I'm* half-northern, that's a stupid remark, David Asher! Just because your professor at medical school came from the north, you've been prejudiced against people like me ever since!'

'Sorry, you know I didn't mean it like that, darling. It's just that he gets up my nose. He's so full of marvellous ideas and doesn't stop to think where the money's coming from. At least I could *talk* to old Ivor, but this new chap's deaf,' he grumbled, and Lucy wanted to assure him that Joe wasn't really like that, but there was nothing she could say. That David knew she and Joe had met before was enough—there was no need to fill him in with the details!

Head bent, David strolled along beside her, and Lucy sought for some way to reassure him about her dinner with the consultant. True, it was unusual for a man as important as Joe Kingsley to invite a mere staff nurse to dine, even if it was purely for professional reasons, but their circumstances were different, she argued with herself. Though not *that* different, she went on silently. You *are* only a staff nurse. The fact that you and Joe were——

'Not sulking, are you?' David's voice broke in on her secret thoughts, and before she could reply he had taken her into his arms, his warm mouth coming down on hers.

For a moment she didn't respond, couldn't respond, her mind too full of another very different man. Then she relaxed, letting David see how much she cared for him.

It didn't work, and he abruptly let her go. They were in the extensive grounds of the Weston, strolling along a little-used path towards the private wing, where David was attending a seminar.

They stood, facing each other, and Lucy's eyes were sad, wondering if this was the beginning of the end for them. 'Please, David, I'm sorry, but I've had a rough day. I'll ring you after I've had dinner with the chief and tell you all about it—will that do?' She put her head on one side, her lips curved in a slight smile, and David groaned, before reaching for her again.

She went willingly enough into his arms this time, unaware of the tall man who was also taking the short cut, but in the opposite direction. Joe Kingsley paused for a moment, then, shrugging, silently retraced his steps.

'This Mr Noble, sir.' Lucy held out the patient's case-notes. 'Will he be staying in the area? He's from Newcastle, and——'

'A good Geordie name,' Joe said, a smile in his voice. 'There's an old ballad about a Noble—Hobbie

Noble: "Now Hobbie was an English man, In Bewcastle dale was bred and born; But his misdeeds they were sae great, They banish'd him ne'er to return." ' Joe quoted, and Lucy tried not to laugh, but gave up the attempt, and they laughed into each other's eyes for a moment before Lucy recollected where they were, and, more importantly, who Joe was.

'Would you like me to call on him once he's back in his lodgings, or. . .?' She let the sentence trail off, aware of the strain between them. For a moment there, they were friends sharing a joke, but now they were back to professor of surgery and liaison nurse.

Joe's eyes bored into hers, and Lucy shifted uncomfortably, moving first one foot then the other. Then he smiled and the sun came out from behind a big dark cloud, and Lucy basked in its warmth.

'We can't ignore the past, can we, little Lucy?' Joe said reflectively, and she shook her head, the bright curls dancing.

'There's no reason why we can't work efficiently together though,' she assured him, hoping she would be proved right. 'Whatever there may have been between us once,' she went on, choosing her words with care, 'doesn't really matter, because it's all quite dead now.'

If she had expected him to comment, she was to be disappointed. 'Mr Tom Noble,' he said instead, frowning down at the notes. 'He's healing well, but he isn't making the progress he ought to be.' He glanced over at her, his eyes expressionless. 'Have a chat with him; see what's eating him. Maybe it's just loneliness—he's missing the friendly Geordie folk. See what you can do, Staff Nurse,' Joe went on brusquely.

Lucy's eyes followed him as he reached for the telephone, then she grabbed the case-notes and hurried out. Because of the unexpected warm spell, Joe was casually dressed today. Gone was the executive-style suit of dark grey that he usually favoured, and in its place was what he had once described as his off-duty clothes; a cream shirt and cords, his casual jacket being thrown over the back of his chair. Whatever he wore, he was an attractive man—no, 'arresting' was more the word, Lucy decided, as she reached the corridor. And tonight she was to dine with him—would he be once more the senior consultant in surgery, or would he revert to the Joe she had once known and loved? She hoped it would be the former, because when Joe put himself out to be pleasant he could be very irresistible indeed!

Lucy found Mr Noble in men's surgical, Shakespeare ward. He was sitting in the day-room, lethargically turning over the pages of an old magazine, and she sat beside him, taking his hand. He was only in his late sixties, but looked older, his sparse grey hair, mottled complexion and shuffling gait giving him a neglected appearance. Since he lived in lodgings on the outskirts of the town and had no one to care whether he ate or slept enough, he probably *was* neglected, Lucy mused as she sought for some topic of conversation, the most likely topic—that of his impending discharge from hospital—being forbidden, since even the slightest suggestion that he might leave was enough to agitate him.

'Do you remember me, Mr Noble? I'm Professor Kingsley's liaison nurse,' she began, and the patient gazed blankly at her, then shook his head firmly, but

Lucy thought he remembered her perfectly well. Perhaps, like Joe Kingsley's, his was a highly selective
memory! 'The professor wondered whether there was
anything I could get you—I'm out and about quite a
lot, and there might be something you want in the
shops. I'm off to Warwick shortly,' she added, and Mr
Noble ruminated for a moment, then shook his head
again. 'I'll go, then,' Lucy sighed, gathering up her
bag. 'I see from your notes that you were born in
Newcastle—that's where my mother comes from. She's
gone back there to live, as a matter of fact,' she went
on, pretending no interest in his answer as she rum-
maged about in her bag.

'Oh, aye? In the town itself, like?' At last there was
a spark of interest, and Lucy hastened to follow it up.

'She was born in Newcastle but she lives out in the
wilds now, in a village called Newhope. Do you know
that part, Mr Noble?'

He shook his head. 'No, I've not been further than
Hexham; I was married there,' he muttered, half to
himself.

'Have you any relatives living there now?' Lucy
asked, wondering whether they might be able to re-
settle him nearer his boyhood home; but, although he
screwed up his face in thought and appeared genuinely
to be trying to remember, Mr Noble decided that there
wouldn't be anyone left of his family.

'We were thirteen at one time, but eleven died; that
I *do* know,' he rumbled on. 'That'd leave me and wor
Eleanor, but I. . .' He shrugged, then closed his eyes,
and Lucy left him to think things over. She knew he
had no children, but if his sister was younger than him
there was a good chance she was still living, and there

was no harm in making enquiries. She considered that trying to make patients happy was all part of her job, and hoped Joe would agree with her.

'Lucy! Dear Lucy—where *have* you been?'

Lucy turned quickly, Heather's ringing tones being unmistakable, and they hugged each other. 'I've been looking for you on and off,' Lucy admitted, and Heather pursed her lips.

'Must must have been more off than on, then! That new sister keeps telling me you're off visiting, so, sad of eye, I make my lonely way back to the nurses' home,' Heather said in a voice that quivered, and Lucy chuckled. 'Your job sounds glamorous, anyway,' Heather went on. 'All that out and about, visiting folk in their own homes—wish I could get a job like that.'

Lucy was aware of her friend's sharp gaze. If she'd been given the sister's post, she had intended asking for Heather as her staff nurse, but as it was. . . 'Are you interested in the home-care scheme, then?' If Heather had a genuine interest it might be possible to put her name forward. It would be fun working together again.

'We-ll,' Heather considered, 'it might be rather fun. More interesting than paeds, anyway. You wouldn't believe the awful pranks some of those kids get up to!'

'You like children, you know you do. Wouldn't you find my job rather boring after a while?' They were outside Arden ward now, where their ways parted, and Lucy was anxious to be out and about again.

Heather's eyes glinted with mischief. 'I might not find your new consultant boring! Didn't I tell you about his lovely black eyes? What's he like to work for? You haven't really told me,' she rushed on, and Lucy hesitated.

'He's very hardworking,' she said at last, 'and very fair. I——'

'Is *that* all you can say about him?' Heather howled. 'Half the nurses here are madly in love with him, and I'd like the chance to get to know him better. Of course, he——'

'Professor Kingsley is married,' Lucy said, determined to squash *that* line of thought straight away! 'Come to my room tonight and we'll have a good—— Oh, sorry, no I can't.' Belatedly she remembered her dinner with Joe. 'Tomorrow night,' she amended, but Heather shook her head, her long face doleful.

'Can't. I'm on days off and I'm going home, then it's nights—you could come to see me there, couldn't you?' she suggested, and Lucy promised to do so.

'I'll see you, then—bye!' she called, but Heather clutched her bag, forcing Lucy to turn round.

'Why can't you manage it tonight? Are you going somewhere exiting? Come on, you can tell me—I thought we were friends.' Heather pouted, her face eager.

'As a matter of fact, I'm dining with Paul Newman and Robert Redford—oh, and Charles Dance might look in, too. I must go now!' With a final wave, a relieved Lucy darted into the safety of her ward. If Heather were to find out that she was dining with Joe Kingsley. . .

It was a busy day for Lucy and she half hoped that Joe would cancel their dinner date. A quiet evening in would suit her very well.

Her last patient for the day presented her with the

most taxing problem of all. Although the scheme was intended primarily for surgical patients, Joe hadn't ruled out certain medical conditions, and it was on Wilmcote ward, women's medical, that Lucy found Carol Barrett. She was only two years older than Lucy but seemed to have lived half a lifetime longer. Carol had been married and divorced twice and had, until recently, been living with her boyfriend and taking care of his children. Now she was on her own again, since the boyfriend refused to take her back, claiming that she was a bad influence on the children.

Lucy conceded that he could be right, since Carol had been exhibiting some bizarre behaviour on the ward. As a teenager in London, she had been diagnosed as schizophrenic, but now had no contact with the psychiatric service and had remained out of hospital for several years.

Whatever happened, Wilmcote would have to keep her at least until Monday. Carol was a long-time sufferer from ulcerative colitis and the symptoms had flared up again at about the time she and her boyfriend were splitting up. Now she had improved physically and, to some degree, mentally as well. While remaining tense and agitated at times, she was coping as well as could be expected. Lucy knew that she was eating normally now and that the signs and symptoms had subsided sufficiently for her to be discharged. Ulcerative colitis was one of those conditions where surgical intervention might be necessary at some stage and she might then become Arden ward's patient, though Lucy doubted that the woman could cope with any more problems.

Carol was pathetically pleased to see her, and

gripped her hand. 'It's nice of you to come back, Nurse Lucy—did you see Nick?'

Lucy shook her head. 'No, but the social worker is going to have a word with him. You might be better off without him, though,' Lucy suggested, and Carol turned startled green eyes on her.

'I never thought. . . No, I'd like to go back, I miss the children. Where will I go till he lets me go back?'

That was where the problem lay. Joe thought Carol might disrupt Arden ward but would have been willing to take her for a few days if it hadn't been for her condition. She could have been nursed in a cubicle by herself, and, as she no longer had to make frequent use of the commode, Lucy didn't think the patients at present on Arden would have been placed at risk, but she saw the force of Joe's arguments. Harry, too, was against admitting the woman, no matter *what* she suffered from.

Between all the social services they should be able to find somewhere for her to live, Lucy thought, and tried to reassure Carol about that before she left. Strictly speaking, Carol wasn't a home-care patient at all; she was more of a social problem, and health care and social care were meant to be kept separate. Joe liked to offer help whenever he could, though, and Lucy's eyes softened. He was a kind, caring doctor, no matter what faults he might have in other ways! She walked thoughtfully back to her own unit. Some people had so many problems it was a wonder they survived at all, and she wished desperately she could do something for Carol.

Sister Shepham glanced up as she hurried in. 'Ah,

there you are, Lucy! The Professor left you a note—I said I wasn't sure if you would be back before I left.'

With fingers that trembled, Lucy took the slim envelope. Wondering if Joe *was* cancelling their dinner date, she slit the envelope open and read the terse note. Then she re-folded it quickly, thrusting it into her shoulder-bag.

'That's one job less,' she commented. 'I popped into see Mr Noble earlier and he thinks he's got a sister living, probably still in Northumberland. Did you want to tell the Professor or shall I?'

'Um, you had better tell him, I think. You've spent more time with Mr Noble than I have. If we can get the man settled back up where he belongs, it might be better in the long run. Oh—what about Mrs Pierson? Have all the facilities been laid on?' Sister went on, and by the time they had finished discussing the various patients Joe was back from his own visits. He stood surveying the pair of them for a moment, then Sister Shepham turned to him with a warm smile, and Lucy felt the unexpected sting of jealousy.

For heaven's sake! How could she possibly be jealous of Edna Shepham?

Joe appeared to notice Lucy for the first time, but his smile was cool and never quite reached his eyes. 'Did you get my note, Staff? Sorry about that,' he said briefly, not giving her a chance to even open her mouth. Then he launched into a description of a patient he had just met, and Lucy forced herself to concentrate. Patients were the reason she was here, after all. The fact that Joe had cancelled their dinner date without even offering an excuse was really of no importance whatsoever.

Since her evening stretched long and lonely ahead, Lucy decided to go home instead, ringing her father first to alert him. As she drove slowly along the winding road she found herself wondering exactly *why* Joe had cancelled their evening out. His note was blunt to the point of rudeness. But hadn't he always been like that? Some things never changed.

Her father was full of plans for the future. 'Your mother's been on the blower again, Lucy. That's twice this week,' he rushed on, insisting upon making her a cup of tea she didn't really want. 'And Sadie's coming down—that's definite. She can have the room you've always had,' he went on, not noticing the look of distress that crossed Lucy's face.

The hospital had let her retain her room, but living in one room was less than ideal, and she had developed a yearning for her own home. Wondering where Joe was living now, she murmured that yes, the room she'd always had would be ideal for Sadie. 'I expect she'll need more space than I do, though. She'll be bringing her ghetto-blaster down with her, then there'll be loads of clothes that she simply *can't* manage without!'

Her father chuckled. 'Just like you when you were young, eh? Pity you couldn't move back for a while, though. Still, you've——'

'But I would have!' Lucy exclaimed. 'Oh, Dad, I did suggest it—just for the six months this new job will last, but then you said Sadie was coming to stay and——'

'There's room enough for the two of you! There's the spare bedroom! Sadie can have that and you can keep your old room. What do you say?' His face was eager, the years dropping away from him, and Lucy hugged him, then shook her head.

'No, it wouldn't work out, Dad. There simply wouldn't be enough room for two women in this house! We would get under each other's feet and Sadie's only eighteen—she probably would——'

'Of course it would work! I'd be glad if you'd come home, just for a little while—will you, dear?'

She couldn't ignore the plea in his eyes. 'All right, I'd like that, but Sadie must have my room; it's bigger and there'll be plenty of room for all her gear! I'll take the spare room. I might as well have a look at it now.'

Lucy made her way slowly upstairs, wondering if two extra might be more than her father could stand.

She stood in the centre of the small spare room, gazing about her with dismay. It wasn't until now that she realised just *how* small it was. There was scarcely room for the narrow bed, single wardrobe and dressing-table. Where on earth would she hang her duty clothes? She received an allowance for wearing her own clothes, so had decided to do so, buying a couple of neat summer suits to see her through until the autumn, plus a selection of tops. There might be a time when she would actually resume ward nursing, so she had retained her uniform dresses, and she liked to keep them separate. Even her room at the hospital was bigger than this one!

Wearily she sank on to the bed, her thoughts sombre. There wasn't room for her here, and there wasn't room of any sort for her in Joe Kingsley's heart either. Why *had* he cancelled their dinner? That still rankled, no matter how much she tried to rationalise it. He was a busy man; perhaps some surgical problem had come up and he knew he wouldn't make it on time. Yes, that was probably it, but he could at least have mentioned it in the note. He——

'Lucy! Visitor for you, dear. I'm just giving him a nice cup of tea.' Her father's voice startled her, and for a second Lucy wondered where she was. She sat up, yawning, then gazed about her blankly, wondering what she was doing in the cheerless spare room. Then she realised she must have dozed off.

'I'm coming, Dad.' She hurried down the stairs, wondering how David had found the time to call. Despite the fact that he had more time off now, his new 'old man' kept him busy and he never seemed to know when he would be free. It was good of him to spend some of his precious free time driving out to see her, though, and Lucy's smile was warm as she entered the cosy sitting-room, where her father was dispensing tea and cakes—not to David Asher, but to the 'old man' himself.

Joe Kingsley rose at her precipitate entrance, his eyes narrowing as the smile left Lucy's face.

CHAPTER FOUR

'Oh, it's you, Professor.' Lucy tried to sound welcoming, but probably failed abysmally. 'Do sit down, won't you?' she said, seating herself beside her father on the settee, leaving Joe to resume his lonely seat opposite.

Her father must have sensed the tenseness in the atmosphere, for he gave what Lucy knew to be his embarrassed chuckle. 'Been warm of late,' he muttered, and Joe gravely agreed that it had. Lucy didn't comment. Instead she made a great show of stirring her tea, despite the fact that she didn't take sugar. What on earth did Joe want?

'Very tasty,' Joe commented, as he took another bite of the cake her father had brought out. 'Not home-made, is it?'

Lucy shook her head, and saw Joe's eyes follow the movement. 'No, I haven't time for baking at the moment, but——'

'Sadie loves baking!' her father put in enthusiastically, and Lucy smiled.

'Yes, so you said. She'll be able to provide plenty of home-made goodies for you while she's here.' Her voice warmed when she spoke to her father, and she hoped Joe Kingsley noticed the difference. 'Sadie's my stepsister,' she added for Joe's benefit.

'Her mother and me—well, we drifted apart, Professor,' Mr Powell put in mildly. 'Even got ourselves divorced. Don't hold with it myself, but there

55

you are. . .' He shrugged, as if to say 'that's women for you', then went on, 'Any old how, to cut a long story short, Margaret went back up north and I stayed here. That was a while back. She. . .' He paused, obviously finding it difficult to talk about his ex-wife's remarriage, and Lucy helped him out.

'My mother remarried, Professor Kingsley, then her husband had a fatal heart attack, and she may be coming back—just for a visit, of course,' she rushed on. She didn't want her father to build up his hopes of her mother's returning for good, for Lucy was convinced she never would. The wounds had gone too deep for that, and not even drastic surgery could mend their marriage. 'My mother's husband had a daughter, Sadie, and she's coming to visit with us for a little while. She's eighteen and taking a year off before deciding what she wants to do,' she added haltingly. Of course she welcomed the visit, wanted to get to know the girl better, but there was no doubt that Sadie had taken her own place in her mother's affections and that hurt, just a little. In addition, Sadie seemed to be a paragon of all the virtues—she loved baking, sewed like a dream, and was only too eager to help the sick, the halt and the lame wherever they could be found.

'Will she follow you into the nursing profession?' Joe asked with interest, watching the varied emotions crossing Lucy's face.

'Yes, I suppose she might,' she replied, surprised by the thought. 'She loves helping people, and——'

'Then I'll have *two* girls in the caring profession!' her father said proudly, with what Joe privately thought was a glaring lack of tact. Couldn't he see how painful it was for his only daughter to come to terms with the fact that she had to share her parents with another daughter? Probably not, Joe conceded, getting up, only too well aware that his spur-of-the-moment visit had gained him nothing.

Lucy forced herself to see him to the door. After all, it was what a good hostess would do. Sadie would undoubtedly do so, she thought gloomily as she opened the door for him.

'Don't take it too much to heart, little Lucy. I don't think your father realises how difficult it's going to be for you,' Joe said unexpectedly, and her eyes widened in dismay. Was it that obvious?

'I can't think what you mean, Professor,' she said stubbornly, and Joe's eyes glinted for a moment, causing Lucy to wonder if she'd gone too far.

'It was Joe once,' was all the comment he made, then turned just as Lucy thought she could safely close the door. 'I'm sorry about our dinner date, but something came up and I knew I'd be late. It was a domestic matter,' he went on with some reluctance, then sketched a salute before leaving.

Lucy closed the door firmly, before leaning against it for a moment. A domestic matter. That could mean only one thing—he was living with his wife again and she had objected to his taking out a member of his staff, a *female* member of staff. What Mrs Kingsley would say if she knew exactly how close her husband and Staff Nurse Powell had been was anybody's guess. She would certainly have good reason then for not wanting him to take that very same staff nurse out to dinner!

* * *

'At least we've *one* more patient now.' Sister's Shepham's voice was disapproving, and Lucy knew she liked to keep busy. Having only five patients on Arden ward wasn't to Lucy's liking either, but at least she got the chance to get out and about, while poor Edna Shepham was stuck in the hospital.

'I can't think what the new doctor will find to do once she arrives,' the ward sister went on, staring down at the new patient's case-notes. 'Joe says she's very keen, very enthusiastic, but then Americans always are. I expect she'll turn the place over, trying to re-schedule everything,' she said gloomily.

'She'll be as cross as you are, with so little to do,' Lucy put in, thankful that she wouldn't see much of Dr Harriet Hamilton. The way Joe raved about her, you would think she was in the world's top ten as far as surgeons went. Privately she wondered whether Dr Hamilton and Joe had had an affair when he had worked out there.

'I must fly, Edna; sorry I can't help you with all your tasks! I've got to be back before two,' Lucy went on, aware that Joe was doing a ward round in the professional unit and that she was expected to be present. Why she couldn't think, but there had been a note in her pigeon-hole, instructing her to present herself on the small ward attached to women's surgical.

She was in good time for her visit to Cordelia ward, an offshoot of women's surgical which was named, somewhat predictably, Hathaway. Wherever you went there was the Shakespeare connection, she thought wryly. Here Joe kept those patients under his own care, whereas the main surgical wards were shared with other consultants. Once Dr Hamilton had arrived he would probably spend more time on Cordelia, leaving her to get the home-care scheme properly underway.

Wondering what it would be like working under a female consultant, Lucy walked into the ward and began chatting to the ladies. Two of the patients in here would be discharged early, under the home-care project, and she had already met one of them.

Mrs Welford suffered from epilepsy, though she was under Joe's care because of her gall bladder operation. She was a remarkably cheerful woman, and waved to Lucy, then indicated her lockerful of get-well cards.

'You wouldn't think I was that popular, would you, Nurse? And that's a fact! Folk don't always appreciate their mother until she's ill,' she added darkly, and Lucy chuckled.

'It's only when they have to pick up after themselves and find that the home laundry service doesn't work automatically that they realise how much they care for old Mum!' Lucy agreed, picking up each card and reading the loving messages. Mrs Welford had seven grandchildren, and every one had sent her a card, some of them hand-made.

Lucy was just reading the last one when her sixth sense warned her of Joe's approach. Soft-footed and alone, he approached the bed, and Mrs Welford's face lit up. It was amazing, Lucy thought, how much the sight of Joe made even the most gravely ill patient feel better! Once he'd had that effect on her, but not any more, she decided, giving him a direct look.

'I'm glad to see you looking so much better, Mrs Welford—Sister tells me you're raring to get home,' Joe began gently, and the patient beamed.

'Well, I've only the one son living at home now, and

he and my old man manage well enough, I suppose, but it's better to be there,' Mrs Welford confided. 'They keep a-coming in, asking me all sorts of questions,' she went on, 'like where do I keep the clean tablecloths, and suchlike, and I do wonder what state my house'll be in when I get home!'

Joe threw back his head and laughed, and Lucy closed her eyes in dismay. She hated it when he laughed like that; it brought back too many memories—memories better left unresurrected.

Then the bad moment was past, and Lucy glanced up to see the Cordelia ward sister approaching, together with Edna Shepham and a tall slender woman in a white coat.

'Hello there, Professor! I see you're charming the girls as usual!' The woman greeted Joe with a big smile, and he got up, chuckling.

'Ah, there you are—ladies,' he addressed the patients, 'this is my secret weapon from the States—Dr Harriet Hamilton.'

Dr Hamilton made a slight curtsy, her merry face alight with laughter, her bright orange curls bobbing. So this was Harriet Hamilton! She was older than Lucy had expected, nearer forty than thirty, and certainly not a raving beauty. A pleasantly round face was topped by the curls, the colour of which owed nothing to nature, then Lucy became aware that shrewd grey eyes were assessing her even as she was assessing Dr Hamilton!

'Harry, this is Lucy Powell; she's my liaison nurse on Arden.' Joe made the introductions, then stepped back, a slight smile hovering about his mouth.

'Hello, Lucy. Joe's told me a lot about you.' Dr

Hamilton greeted her warmly enough, and Lucy managed a startled smile, wondering what exactly Joe had said about her.

When they had finished the round, they trooped into sister's office for a pot of tea, and Lucy found herself sitting next to Dr Hamilton, who smilingly made room for her.

'Joe's been telling me how enthusiastic you are about the home-care scheme. I'm glad,' she said simply, and Lucy warmed to her.

'Being in hospital is abnormal; the patients' lives are outside, in their own homes,' Lucy said, accepting a cup of tea.

'I agree, but not everybody sees it that way. There's a lot of opposition to this scheme—am I right?' Dr Hamilton demanded.

'You two ladies are deep in conversation—I hope it isn't girl-talk,' Joe broke in, his smile warm as it rested on Dr Hamilton.

'I'm tempted to say it was, just to annoy you, Joe, but I won't,' the woman parried. 'We were talking about the resistance to the home-care scheme.'

'Some nurses in the community don't like the idea at all,' Joe agreed. 'They think it's a good enough idea in theory, but that it won't work in practice; that the patients will be the ones to suffer. We have to convince them that it won't be so,' he asserted, and there were murmurings of agreement. 'The main objection seems to be that we're creaming off the best of the patients, principally the younger ones, and leaving the district nurses with the old handicapped folk. And I suppose there *is* some truth in that,' he went on thoughtfully, 'though at the moment we're getting too many of the over-sixties. Then they're concerned that the patients will become confused—having ten days of our home-care nurses, then being transferred to their usual district nurse. We'll have to get the district nurses more involved in the selection of patients, I think.'

Lucy liked to study his face when his interest was aroused in whatever subject. His normally stern features became animated, his eyes glowed with a dark fire she found arresting, his hard mouth became more mobile, what she thought of as a sensuous lower lip jutted out, and every now and again, as now, he licked that lower lip, his tongue darting in and out. . . Hoping she wasn't blushing at her own memories, Lucy fought for control, struggling to catch up with what Joe was actually saying, rather than what he had once said to her in the past.

The talk had turned to staffing levels by the time she had collected her wits, and her first thought was of Heather. Perhaps now wasn't the time to mention her, but she could at least let Joe know that there was a staff nurse only too willing to join his scheme!

'When Arden's running as we want it,' Joe was saying, 'we ought to have another staff nurse, a ward-based one,' he went on, glancing over at Lucy. 'Is there anyone on the staff that you know of who might be interested?'

'There's Nurse Baynes, sir—she works on children's at the moment.'

'You can't mean that madcap Heather Baynes, surely, Nurse? She hasn't a sensible thought in her head,' the ward sister said disapprovingly, and Lucy's face fell.

'Perhaps we'll have Sister Shepham make a short-list,' Joe suggested, 'and we can include Nurse Baynes.'

The meeting broke up and they rose to go, but if Lucy thought she was free of Joe's disturbing influence she was mistaken, for he dropped back, choosing to walk with her rather than with Harriet Hamilton. 'We must have that dinner date, Staff Nurse,' he said, and Lucy showed her surprise.

'Oh, but I thought your——' Hastily she stopped, aware of his sharp glance.

'You thought what, Staff?' he enquired mildly, and Lucy was at a loss to answer.

'I thought your—your domestic upset had. . .' She stopped again, feeling her irritation rise. Surely he didn't need her to spell it out for him? 'I thought you would be too busy in the evenings,' she finally got out, and a reflective smile crossed his face briefly, then was gone.

'Even consultants have to eat. What about Saturday night?' he asked as they paused before going their separate ways.

'Well——' Lucy hesitated, partly because she didn't want to appear too eager, and partly because she knew an evening out with Joe wasn't a good idea '—if you're sure. . .'

'Yes, I'm sure. Saturday it is, then—I think my domestic commitments will allow that,' he added, then strode away towards his next appointment, leaving Lucy to catch up with Harriet Hamilton, who was obviously waiting for her.

'Problems?' the American doctor asked sympatheti-cally, and Lucy smiled to herself. If only she knew!

'No, not really,' she said. 'It was just something Mr Kingsley and I had to sort out.'

'Uh-uh. He has a whole load of problems, but I guess you know that. Suppose you give me a run down on every patient you've seen, Lucy. I'd like to sort them out in my mind,' the doctor went on, and Lucy brought her mind back to surgery, but Dr Hamilton's words came back to haunt her at intervals throughout the day—'He has a whole load of problems.'

Saturday brought Lucy her own load of problems. The coming visit of Sadie Bland had been preying on her mind even though she knew she was letting her imagination run away with her. But what *exactly* would Sadie be like?

She needn't have worried—Sadie's smile was so warm and the girl so obviously glad to see her that Lucy felt guilty. So much so that she rather overdid her welcome, and was aware of her father's startled expression.

'I hope I'll not be a bother to you, Lucy. I'll try to be quiet, like,' Sadie assured her, in only the faintest of north-country accents. She was a tall girl, built on generous lines, with lively blue eyes, her eager expression reminding Lucy vaguely of a new puppy, anxious to please!

'Of course you won't be a bother. Dad and I are looking forward to showing you some of the sights,' Lucy assured her. 'How's Mum?' she asked, as she helped Sadie cram her clothes into what Lucy saw now was an inadequate number of drawers.

'Oh, she's champion!' Sadie said blithely. 'Sends her love, like. She thought she might come down, too, but

she didn't know how you'd take it,' she went on
candidly.

'I don't normally live here, so it wouldn't be any of
my business. Anyway, she's still my mother, so naturally I would be pleased to see her again. It's not as if
she's been away years,' Lucy said slowly, wondering
how it would be to see Mum again. They had never
been close, but your mother was your mother, after
all.

'You've brought enough clothes to last a couple of
years!' Lucy went on, hanging up yet another pair of
designer jeans. Most of the clothes were expensive,
and she gasped as she picked up the last item, a party
dress of iridescent green-gold, with a longish pleated
skirt. 'Oh, Sadie, this is lovely!' Lucy twirled round
with the dress held against her. Of course it was too
long, but the colour suited her even better than it did
the much darker Sadie, and they both giggled.

'Your Mam bought that for me,' Sadie confided, 'on
my last birthday, it was. Do you really like it?' she
went on, her eyes on Lucy's face.

'Mm, I do, very much. We must find you some
parties so that you can wear it. I'll see what the student
nurses have in the way of dances and parties and let
you know,' Lucy offered, reluctantly handing back the
pretty dress.

'You can wear it tonight, if you like,' Sadie offered.
'Stepdad said you were being wined and dined by a
tall, dark and handsome consultant! Go on, wear it,
and he won't be able to resist you!'

'That's sweet of you, but I'm afraid it's a bit dressy
for a quiet dinner. Anyway, it's my boss I'm dining
with—don't start getting romantic notions about my

evening out!' Lucy said lightly, wondering what on earth she *was* going to wear.

In the end she settled on a little dark navy dress, perfectly plain, with a discreet neckline. So plain, in fact, that it cried out for some embellishment—a piece of sparkling jewellery, perhaps, and Lucy was searching in her jewel-box when the doorbell rang. Helping Sadie settle in had made her late with her own preparations, but surely it couldn't be seven yet? A glance at her watch told her it was nearly five to, and that she had better hurry. Being kept waiting wouldn't improve Joe's hair-trigger temper.

She renewed her search but couldn't find what she was looking for—a dainty *diamanté* and pearl brooch that had once belonged to her grandmother. It would have been just the thing to brighten up the dress, but it couldn't be helped. Hurriedly slipping into her high-heeled black shoes, Lucy took a final look at herself in the mirror. Yes, she would do. Her only jewellery was a pair of pearl drop earrings, but that was something, anyway.

She made her unhurried way down the narrow stairs, conscious that it would be bonus points to Joe if she appeared to be anxious to see him. It was exactly seven o'clock as she entered the sitting-room—to find him in animated conversation with Sadie. Pausing a moment to pin a bright smile to her face, Lucy went in, and was glad to see her father's face wreathed in smiles. At least *someone* was pleased to see her!

'You look nice, Lucy, love,' her father said loudly, and Joe broke off his conversation long enough to agree that she did.

'Very nice indeed, Mr Powell. And you're on time,

too,' Joe added. Sadie's gaze was frankly admiring, and that did something for Lucy's self-esteem.

She treated them all to what she hoped was a cool, sophisticated smile, but was disconcerted to find that Joe's eyes were glinting with amusement as he got up from the settee where, Lucy noted, he had been sitting next to Sadie.

'Where are we going?' she asked as they set off. Not too far a drive, she hoped. Once they were in the restaurant everything would be all right, but alone with him in the darkness of a car. . .

'I thought the White Hart—that's where I booked, anyway,' he replied. 'Your stepsister and I have a friend in common, by the way. Do you remember my talking about old Neddy Henderson? He was like a father to me at one time. Young Sadie used to run errands for him until they moved out into the wilds! It's a small world,' Joe commented, a smile in his voice.

Lucy was silent. Yes, she remembered Joe telling her about Mr Henderson, an old shoe repairer with whom the adolescent Joe had spent many happy hours. But that was yesterday, many yesterdays ago when she and Joe were in love—at least, *she* was in love. It was cruel of him to remind her of those days now, or perhaps he didn't mean to be cruel; it was simply that he didn't realise how much she still cared.

Then the discreet lights of the White Hart enveloped them, and Lucy belatedly realised that in Sadie they had a safe topic of conversation, one that could be spun out to last the whole meal if shop-talk petered out.

'So,' Joe said as they sipped their pre-dinner drinks, 'what do you think about Arden ward so far?'

Lucy was surprised at the way her heart lightened because he *didn't* want to talk about Sadie. 'I think it's a wonderful idea, though I wish we had more patients.'

'We will, Lucy, don't worry,' he promised. 'How are you finding your part in all this? That's more to the point,' he added, then dropped his head to study the menu, leaving Lucy free to gaze her fill.

For once, Joe had managed to tame his hair, and it lay smoothed back and neat, though she knew it wouldn't stay that way for long. When he was ruffled or angry, he had this habit of pushing his hair back, then running his fingers through it, ending up with rubbing his hand along the back of his neck, then through his hair again. She had watched him do that so many times that she knew the routine off by heart. Hastily she downed her drink, barely tasting it. The words on the big, leather-covered menu swam before her, and when Joe at last glanced up and silently invited her to choose her meal she had to take another look, and at last the blurred words became legible.

Feeling a fool for taking so long, she decided on prawns in a tomato and wine sauce, followed by steak *garni*. Joe ordered the same for himself, then sat back, his gaze assessing.

'I'm glad you and Sadie have something in common,' Lucy hurriedly broke into the lengthening silence. Joe's gaze was unnerving, to say the least. 'She'll be company for Dad and can tell him how my mother's getting along,' she rushed on. 'She—Sadie, that is—is talking about settling down here but I don't——'

'Must we discuss your little sister?' Joe asked in exasperation. 'Charming and comely though she is, she's hardly an interesting topic of conversation—this is meant to be a working dinner, remember?' he added, his voice hardening, and Lucy nodded, resentful because she had been put in her place.

'Yes, naturally, sir,' she said crisply. 'You were going to tell me about your ideas for a terminal care unit,' she went on, averting her gaze. Then the prawns arrived and there was silence for a few minutes. Lucy's mind was busy even if her voice was silent, and she found she had no appetite for the delicious starter. How she was to cope with the main course, she didn't know. There was still far too much chemistry between them, and coming out this evening had been a mistake, a bad one.

Then Joe startled her by saying, 'Since terminal care is hardly a conversation for the dinner table, let's talk about something else—you, for example.'

Caught unawares, Lucy blurted out, 'But that's why we're here! You wanted to talk about your plans for the future and——'

'Ah, yes, my plans for the future,' Joe agreed solemnly. 'What about *your* plans, Lucy? Will you stay on at the Weston once the trial period's over? I very much hope the post of liaison nurse will become a permanent one, but I can't guarantee it, of course.'

'Of course. I understand that, really, but I'm enjoying it, though I miss bedside nursing, too,' she continued thoughtfully. 'I suppose if I'm honest I'm not really sure what I want to do next,' she confessed.

'And are you honest?' he asked, his eyes on her.

Lucy was thrown off-balance. 'I hope so. Sometimes we lie to ourselves, don't we, and we think we're being honest when we're being nothing of the sort?' she said

sharply, and watched the frown crossing Joe's wide
brow. Then he shrugged.

'You could be right. So, try to be honest and tell me
where you think your future lies,' he went on, apparently unruffled by her remark.

'Naturally I hope to become a ward sister, even if
Mr Browne *does* think I look too young! That's enough
about me; what about you? For how long will the
Weston General satisfy you? Surely you want to go
back to London?' She didn't really want to hear his
plans for the future, was afraid that he would mention
Rosemary, tell her that all was well in his marriage,
but he didn't. Instead, he began on his steak, apparently trying to decide what to tell her and what to keep
back.

'I expect I'll move on once the rehab scheme is
working well,' he acknowledged after a moment. 'I'd
like to spend at least three years here, though. I like
the area, I'm near enough to the theatre to go every
week if I want to, and the job's a challenge. Is that
what it is for you?'

Their eyes met, and Lucy found she couldn't look
away this time. She was mesmerised as his gaze held
on to hers, willing some response from her, but what
she had no way of knowing. 'We all need a challenge,'
she said quietly, and Joe nodded, unaware that it was
he himself who constituted the challenge in her life.

Eventually the talk shifted round to family life, and
Lucy thought that it was Joe who mentioned Sadie, but
it might have been her. Once she was home and back
in the spare room, she wouldn't be able to think
straight, let alone recall who had said what.

'I expect Sadie will stay for a while, but she'll

probably miss her friends before long,' Lucy admitted, as they began on the pudding.

'She'll make new ones,' Joe said dismissively. 'She's young and extrovert enough to do that. You might find she's moved in for good.'

Lucy shrugged. 'The thought isn't *that* unpalatable, you know. Of course I suppose I might resent her a bit, but she's such a lovely girl, so kind and eager to please—a bit like an overgrown puppy! I couldn't *not* like her, and I'm sorry if it seems that way.'

'No, it doesn't, little Lucy. You've a warm heart.' Joe's words were unexpected, and she flushed.

'Thank you for the compliment, but please don't keep calling me "little Lucy"—she died a few years back,' Lucy went on bleakly, pushing aside the last of the sorbet, and refusing Joe's offer of coffee. 'I really ought to be getting back. I expect my father's tired and Sadie will——'

'Leave her to cope!' Joe's voice was sharp. 'She'll manage your father, never fear. He seems well recovered from his CVA.'

'Yes, yes, he is, and he's livened up considerably since we heard Sadie was coming, and there's my mother——' She hesitated, then went on quickly, 'Mum might be coming back, just for a visit, but my father hopes it will be permanent, that they can get back to where they were before the marriage failed. He expects to turn back the clock.' Her smile was bitter.

'You can never do that, Lucy; it isn't good for the clock springs to go backwards.' Joe heaved a sigh, and Lucy wondered whether his own marriage was floundering again. He hadn't mentioned Rosemary once during the evening, but surely they must be together again? And if they were? Then she was back to square one—going out with a married man when her whole upbringing rebelled against such an idea.

Joe's gaze was bleak as it met her own speculative one. 'If we're not having coffee, we'd best get home. I've some papers to work on tomorrow morning and I can't lie a-bed even though it's Sunday!'

'Do you live in Stratford now?' Lucy asked as he opened the car door.

'No, I've a house over at Hadfield, but the hospital provides me with a flat and I use that mostly,' he added, settling himself next to her. He stared into space for a moment, his long fingers idling on the steering-wheel. 'Did I say how fetching you look in that dress? I don't suppose I did—I'm not much of a one to pay fancy compliments these days. I'm getting too old now, I expect,' he went on, and Lucy opened her mouth to protest, then closed it again.

Joe's words had emphasised the gap that existed between them—not only the age-gap, but the maturity gap. She felt she ought to make some comment, but didn't know what to say, beyond thanking him for the compliment, which she did sincerely. 'I spent ages searching for a suitable brooch to wear with it. I've got one my grandmother left me. It's rather pretty, a circle of little pearls and *diamanté*, with a bigger pearl in the middle, but I couldn't find it anywhere. I thought the dress too plain.'

'I like it as it is,' Joe said unexpectedly. 'Too many women dress up with enough baubles to hang on a Christmas tree!'

A little smile played about the corners of Lucy's

mouth. Despite not fishing for a compliment, she was glad she'd got one!

'You're quiet, Lucy,' Joe commented a few moments later, and she roused herself.

'I was just thinking about my brooch, wondering if my father had put it away. It's of no great value, I know, but it has sentimental value. I hope I haven't lost it,' she added ruefully. 'I'm not the world's tidiest person!'

'Neither am I!' Joe chuckled, pleased that they could talk without arguing. As long as they kept off personal matters, they could at least enjoy a civilised conversation. Perhaps in time they might even enjoy a platonic friendship. No, never that.

They were almost within sight of the house when he stopped the car, and Lucy tensed, half hoping, half dreading that he would kiss her—or try to, since she fully intended to resist. 'Lucy, I——' Joe began, then stopped, while she waited, wondering what he was trying to say. 'I hope that this evening means we can be friends again?' he said after a lengthy pause, and Lucy's eyes darkened with pain.

Friends? 'Yes, why not?' she said steadily. 'There's no reason why we can't make an effort to get on together. After all, it's the patients who matter, not our personal feelings. The fact that we don't actually like each other ought to have no bearing on our professional relationship,' she found herself saying, though all the while her heart was shouting that it wasn't true—of course they liked each other!

Joe was stunned, and he glanced down at his hands, seeking inspiration. 'I never realised we didn't like each other. When did you come to that conclusion?'

He turned towards her, his gaze quizzical, and Lucy shifted uneasily.

'Well. . .we never could talk for long without arguing,' she said stubbornly.

'They were amiable arguments, Lucy.' He reached for her hand and gently began to run his finger over her pulse spot.

'They may have been sometimes,' she admitted grudgingly, steeling herself not to snatch her hand away. Did he know what he was doing to her? she wondered. Yes, of course he did. Joe Kingsley never did anything without weighing up the consequences first. He was too clever, too much in control of his feelings and everyone else's. He had probably known what he was doing to her heart all those years ago. The man was a monster! She did snatch her hand away then, and heard his sharply indrawn breath.

'There was no need for that, little Lucy—I'm not going to rape you!'

'No, of course you're not! There's no need, is there? Little Lucy was more than willing once upon a time, and you suppose she still is!' Lucy threw at him. 'Well, Lucy's grown up now and she certainly isn't going to waste her love on a—a philanderer!' she hurried on, knowing she was being unreasonable, but hoping her words were hurting him, as his had once hurt her. 'I suppose younger women appeal to you,' she went on, striving for calm but not achieving it. 'They appeal to your innate male vanity—if younger women still want you, then you must be still desirable!'

'Am I desirable? Thank you, Lucy,' Joe said gravely, but there was a hint of laughter in his voice and Lucy longed to throw something at him. Only old Mr

Browne's voice telling her she was too young stopped her. What he had meant was that she was too immature, but surely her urge to slap Joe's face was perfectly resonable? Hadn't he taken her love, all she had to offer, then thrown everything back in her face, leaving her to find out from the grapevine that he had a wife at home?

She couldn't hold back the sob, but it was more a sob of anger than of grief. She hated him, she did! Yet when he gently took her wrist again she didn't resist. She would show him that she no longer cared, no longer felt any stirring of love at his expert touch. For a moment she managed that, even though her heart was quivering away. Then, with a cry of frustration, she was in his arms, arms which opened wide to enfold her then settled themselves possessively around her slender body, her poor quivering heart pressed closely against his.

'Oh, Lucy! If only you knew!' Joe murmured against her hair, and Lucy sniffed, trying to hold back the tears. Yet one managed to escape and began its slow way down her cheek, to be followed by several more. Gently, as each one arrived Joe wiped it away with his finger, Lucy feeling her heart would break again at his touch. 'Poor, poor Lucy,' he went on tenderly, and she snuggled closer, aware of the dangers but uncaring. She was back where she belonged—in the strong arms of Joe Kingsley. The past could be forgotten for the moment. She closed her eyes tightly, trying to keep not only the past but also the future at bay. Whatever she felt for Joe, he belonged to his wife. She had a duty to the woman to pull away from his embrace, sit up and smile calmly and tell him his technique had improved.

So why didn't she? Think of Rosemary, she told herself, moaning quietly as Joe's hands began a leisurely exploration of her body. Think of Rosemary. . .

Weakly she struggled against him, and to her surprise Joe let her go immediately. Face flushed, hair awry, and lipstick smudged, she fought for breath, anxious to tell him exactly what she thought of him.

'I'm sorry, Lucy—that should never have happened.' Joe's voice was bitter, and all the words she wanted to say left Lucy's mind. Her brain wasn't functioning as it should, and all she could think of was that Joe didn't want her any more.

'That's all right, we all get carried away sometimes!' Lucy's voice was as bitter as his, and she pulled her shawl tightly about her, her body cooling rapidly, her heart firmly set in a block of ice. It must have been, for she felt so cold.

Instead of avoiding her censorious gaze and starting up the car again, eager to get her home, Joe shifted restlessly in his seat, then their eyes met. In their depths Lucy saw as much misery as there was in her own. 'Nothing like that will ever happen again, I promise. Now I'd better get you home—your father and Sadie will be worrying.'

It was only moments later that they drew up outside her father's house, Joe brusquely refusing her offer of coffee. Lucy got out and forced herself to walk steadily up to the porch. She didn't look back, yet her ears were waiting for the sound of the car engine, and she didn't hear the car leave until the door was opened and Sadie was greeting her.

'Oh, is Mr Kingsley not coming in? I've had the pot warming this half-hour or more!'

Lucy felt Sadie's disappointment keenly, the more so because she herself shared it. 'No, he had to rush back,' she explained, then was forced to sip the tea Sadie placed in front of her, trying to answer the girl's questions about the dinner, the restaurant, what she and Joe had talked about. Then she shook her head, trying to clear it. She was over-tired, she knew, but surely she wasn't imagining that her pretty pearl brooch was pinned to the front of Sadie's silk blouse?

'That brooch. . .' Lucy began hesitatingly. 'It's very pretty,' she hurried on, as Sadie beamed at her.

'It's lovely, isn't it? Stepdad gave it to me! He said it belonged to your grandmother and it was such a lovely piece it ought to be worn more. He said you'd worn it once or twice but hadn't bothered with it for ages, so it would be all right for me to have it—is it all right? If it's yours, then you must have it back.' Head bent, Sadie began unfastening the safety chain, while Lucy looked on, aghast. Her brooch!

'There we are, safe and sound.' With a flourish, Sadie placed the brooch in Lucy's hand. 'I expect Stepdad thought you'd finished with it. Don't worry, I've plenty of jewels, really, only——'

'No, of course you must have it, Sadie! It's true, I haven't worn it in ages, and Dad must have thought I didn't want it any more. Go on, I'd like you to wear it,' Lucy assured her. Of course, she was in the right and Sadie would understand if she wanted to take the brooch back, but it would be selfish to do so since the girl was clearly made up with it. And it suits her better than it does me, Lucy thought honestly as she pinned it back on to the blouse.

'Well, if you're sure. . .' Sadie said slowly, and impulsively Lucy kissed her on the brow.

'Of course I'm sure, dear. We're going to be sisters, aren't we? Now I'm going to be selfish and leave you with the washing-up, for I'm asleep on my feet!' she went on lightly, anxious to get up to the sanctuary of her room before a further crop of tears started. Already she could feel them building up at the backs of her eyes. 'See you in the morning! Oh—is Dad all right? That shows you how tired I am, forgetting to ask after him!'

'Aye, he's champion, Lucy. Really fine. Don't you worry about washing the cups—I'll see to them. Up you go to bed and dream about your handsome Mr Kingsley!'

Feeling that she'd had enough trauma to last her all month, let alone all day, Lucy walked slowly up the narrow stairs to the spare room. By artificial light it looked even smaller and even less homely, but at least it was private, and she carefully unzipped the much-cherished dress, kicked off her shoes, then threw herself on to the bed, not even bothing to remove her make-up or clean her teeth. All she wanted was sleep, oblivion. . .

But sleep wouldn't come. She closed her eyes and tried to empty her mind, but all she could see in the darkness was Joe Kingsley smiling down at her, a younger Joe, the man she had once known, once loved. . .

It was at a birthday party thrown by one of the doctors that she had first seen him. Of course she had been aware of him before—he wasn't a man to be ignored, with his tall lean, athletic body, his black hair and eyes, lazy smile and, surprisingly, his dedication to duty. Despite being a senior registrar, he worked harder than any houseman Lucy knew, and never seemed to need sleep. If there was a crisis and they were short of doctors, Joe could always be relied upon to fill in, could always be trusted.

That evening he had been escorting a vibrant red-head, who clung to him for the first part of the evening. Then, when a wistful-eyed Lucy had looked for them again, Joe had been on his own, chatting easily to one of the staff nurses, his smile for her alone. Lucy had sighed, wishing she could be the recipient of that sensuous smile, feel those dark eyes glowing just for her. Then, shrugging, she had turned aside as her own escort, a fellow student, had claimed her for what proved to be an energetic new dance, one which left her gasping for breath.

Then Joe had cut in, whisking her away, getting her a drink, which her escort had neglected to do, and standing talking to her, of all people! The charismatic Joe Kingsley actually talking to *her*!

Lucy groaned, trying to shut out the memory. What was the use of dwelling on the past? Nothing good ever came of that. What mattered now was the present and the future. She smiled into the darkness, her mind drifting back again, despite her efforts to sleep. That meeting had been followed by many others. And Joe, to her great relief, had proved to be a perfect gentle-man. Not for him the fumbling in the back-seat of a car, a roving hand making demands upon her that she didn't want, couldn't cope with. No, he had behaved impeccably, until that final night. . .

That night she had given not only her heart but also her body to Joe Kingsley, with no thought of the morrow, no thought that Joe's love for her was any less than her own for him. It wasn't until the hospital grapevine had started sending out messages that she understood the truth of what had happened: Joe was a married man. What was more, he was still living with his wife—hadn't her ward sister seen them out together?

She had given him her all, believed his words of love—oh, yes, he had claimed to love her. That was the bitterest blow of all. He had lied to her and cheated his wife—could anyone be more despicable than that?

That last scene wouldn't be denied, and Lucy lived through it again, as she tossed and turned on top of the uncomfortable bed, the tears flowing. Wallowing in self-pity was alien to her nature, and at length the tears stopped and she sat up, reaching for a tissue. After she had wiped her eyes and blown her nose she felt drained, so inutterably weary, that she lay down again.

If only Joe had defended himself! Or, even better, apologised for what he had done to her. Of course, she had been willing enough—Lucy acknowledged that now even if she hadn't been able to then. Yet Joe had said nothing, beyond telling her that he had meant what he said, that he *did* care for her. Yet he had given her no other words of comfort that she could cling to in the bleak days ahead—only told her he would stand by her if she should be pregnant. Hardly the words of a romantic hero, yet it was something, at least. And for a few weeks she had cherished the notion that perhaps she might be pregnant, carrying Joe's child, and that everything would come right once she told him. He would divorce his wife, marry her and they would live happily ever after. How naïve that sounded now!

Lucy helped herself to another tissue, taking the box into bed beside her. Of course she hadn't been pregnant, and no doubt Joe had been as relieved as she had at the knowledge. Not that he had asked, beyond a slight raising of a brow when she had met him unexpectedly in the hospital lift one morning. She had shaken her head wordlessly, her heart breaking anew at the expression of relief that had crossed the granite face in front of her. No words were necessary—Joe had offered to take responsibility, and her silence had told him it wasn't necessary.

'Oh, Joe, Joe,' she whispered, clutching the box of tissues to her. She repeated his name over and over again, acknowledging that she still loved Joe Kingsley, despite everything, that she still wanted him back, on any terms. Tonight had shown her that her dream was as empty as the dream of the little student nurse that night, the little Lucy she had once been. She was still naïve and stupid, still searching for that white knight— only he didn't exist. Perhaps he had never existed.

CHAPTER FIVE

'HERE you are, then!' a familiar voice hailed Lucy, and she turned, her smile for David Asher warmer than it had been of late. Since that half-proposal, she had tried to cool the relationship, letting him see that, much as she liked him and enjoyed his company, there was really no more to it than that. She didn't love him, and without love there was no point in getting married. She sensed, too, that David was relieved by her no-non-sense attitude.

'You're always deep in thought these days, my pet,' David said, ruffling her hair affectionately, and Lucy schooled herself not to brush away his hand.

'Weighty matters, Dr Asher, weighty matters,' she said solemnly, and David looked startled for a moment, before noticing the twinkle in her eye.

'You had me fooled then! Listen, I've had the most marvellous news—you remember that course old Ivor said I could go on?'

'Yes, "A Caring Doctor in the Home" or something, wasn't it?' Lucy teased, but David took her seriously.

'It's called "A Caring Doctor in the Community", actually, but never mind that. Well, he said I—look, we can't talk here,' David went on, taking her by the hand as she went to unlock the car. 'I can't get away this evening but how about lunch tomorrow? I'm free during the afternoon—have a proper meal with me, no canteen stodge!' He gazed down at her earnestly, and Lucy found herself accepting.

She got into her car, wondering what it was that David couldn't talk to her about in the car park. She hoped it wasn't the promotion that he was so earnestly seeking—that would mean he could actually *afford* a wife! Despite coming from a fairly wealthy family, he claimed the right to independence and wouldn't want to be beholden to his family to help support a mortgage, a wife and perhaps a child as well.

A child, David's child. The thought made Lucy grow cold. Now *Joe's* child—that would be a different matter, she thought as she followed the familiar winding country road to her home, where Sadie was waiting to be given a lift into Stratford. Once she'd dropped her off, Lucy intended calling on two patients who lived close by.

When she had let herself into the house she found Sadie and her father in the kitchen eating strawberries and cream and laughing together over a cartoon in the paper. Sadie flushed when she saw Lucy and jumped up, almost knocking over the fruit.

'Careful, love, you'll have that juice all over you,' Dad said tenderly. 'Lucy won't take a whip to you for not being ready. You'll wait a bit, won't you, dear?' he said to Lucy, who nibbled her lip in annoyance.

'If Sadie gets ready now——' she began.

'Sit down and have a few strawberries yourself, dear. You're always rushing about all over the place,' he grumbled. 'And young Sadie saved you some.'

'Thank you, Dad,' Lucy broke in before the flustered girl could comment, 'but I'm on duty and I shouldn't really be here. I don't like to drag you away, Sadie—

why don't you finish your fruit in peace, and I'll pick you up on the way back? There's still plenty of time to go shopping.'

'Oh, aye, thanks, but I'll come with you. Give us a minute, like.' Sadie sped away, and Lucy's father frowned at her.

'There wasn't any call for her to rush away just because you're here,' he complained. There were times when his inability to do all he had enjoyed before wore him down, made him quarrelsome, selfish even, and Lucy saw that this was one of those times.

Sitting down for a moment, she put her arms around him and gave him a hug. 'The sooner Sadie goes, the sooner she'll get back to you—though you could come, if you wanted to,' she offered, but as she had expected he shook his head.

'No, a bit too warm for gadding about, dear. Anyway, Sadie knows what I want. She's a good girl— glad she's come to live with us, are you?' He glanced up at Lucy, who smiled.

'Of course I am! I always wanted a little sister!' Lucy laughed, surprised to find that she *did* look upon Sadie as a sister, even though they had no blood relationship. In turn, Sadie had taken on the burden of running the home, though their daily woman still took care of the housework. Sadie actually enjoyed cooking and sewing, two chores Lucy found boring, and there was no doubt that the girl's bright, sunny personality had transformed her father. All in all it was a good thing, and the only cloud on the horizon was Lucy's fear that Sadie would become bored and take off again. Still, they would face that hurdle when they came to it, Lucy was just deciding, when the girl flew down the stairs and burst into the kitchen, her face alight.

'Your Mr Kingsley! He's come—he's out there! I'll let him in, shall I?' she asked, then rushed out, leaving a dismayed Lucy. Sadie wasn't falling for Joe—was she? Visions of herself at that tender age came to her, and she realised just how easily an impressionable girl *could* fall for Joe. She could do no more than stare wordlessly as a beaming Sadie pranced back into the room, with Joe Kingsley following close behind.

Lucy rose hastily, the certainty that she would be criticised for being at home crowding out the dismaying thoughts about Joe and her stepsister.

Joe's gaze was bland, but she wasn't deceived. If he ticked her off for being here it was no more than her due. She *was* on duty and had no excuse to offer. Attack being the best form of defence that she knew, she showed her surprise at seeing him. 'Can I help you, Professor?' she asked politely, a faint smile touching her mouth.

There was a gleam in Joe's eyes, but he shook his head. 'No, not really,' he admitted. 'I was passing and saw your car, so I thought I'd pop in to say hello to your father.'

'And very welcome you are, too!' her father beamed. 'Sadie and I were just having a bowl of strawberries— she treated me, the little love!'

Lucy might have imagined it, but did Joe's gaze turn just a trifle frosty? 'I'm delighted that you're so well looked after,' was his only comment, then he smiled at Sadie, who was standing beside him, her face flushed, a shy smile on her face. Lucy's heart went out to her. Yet surely Sadie was too sophisticated, too adult to feel the pangs of hero-worship and love that she herself had once felt for Joe?

Hating herself for bringing a cloud to her face but knowing she had no choice, Lucy reminded her that they must be going, and Sadie seemed startled for a moment, as if she had forgotten the shopping. Probably she had, Lucy thought wryly, as the girl blushed to the roots of her hair.

When they drove off Sadie's face was still flushed, her eyes sparkling. The look of a woman in love, Lucy thought, feeling desperately sorry for her, but knowing that nothing she said or did would make the slightest difference—she must learn the harsh lesson for herself.

When Lucy returned to the unit later that day, there was no sign of Joe, but Harriet Hamilton was very much in evidence as she showed a group of community nursing officers around the unit.

Dr Harry beamed at Lucy, who managed a rather wan smile in return. All through the journey to the town, and indeed on the return journey, she'd had to endure Sadie's aimless chatter about everything in general, and about Joe Kingsley in particular, and each time she had uttered his name Lucy had felt a knife turn in her heart.

'Of course, this is just the beginning,' Dr Harry was saying, and Lucy brought her mind back to the business in hand. 'We have big plans for the future, but we have to see how things go, kinda feel our way through the scheme,' Harry went on.

There was a lot of opposition to the scheme, though not as much as Joe had expected. Some community nurses thought that Joe's team was unnecessary, since the patients concerned would eventually be discharged into the community and into the care of their GP and local community nurse. What they apparently couldn't see was that it made hospital beds available more quickly and would do much to shorten in-patient waiting lists once it was fully functional.

'What *I* want to see is——' one nursing officer began, then a pleasant, deep voice broke in.

'What *I* want to see is a nice pot of tea for everyone.' And Joe Kingsley strolled into the common-room, smile at the ready, and Lucy slipped away to get the tea organised. If she knew anything about Joe he would soon have the critics eating out of his hand.

She was only half right, and the discussion went on long past going-home time. She was too interested to want to leave, but saw Sister Shepham glance at the wall clock and give Joe a meaning glance.

'As it's getting on for six o'clock, perhaps we ought to call it a day?' Joe suggested with an urbane smile, and there were expressions of dismay from the visiting nurses. He chuckled at their surprise. 'When you're having fun, how time passes!' he joked, and there was a burst of laughter. The meeting broke up with apparent goodwill on both sides, but Lucy's head had begun to ache as she rehearsed the arguments to herself. Despite her enthusiasm, Sister Shepham hadn't stated their case as well as she might have done, and everything Harry had said had been greeted with a chilly politeness that the woman must have found daunting.

Harry shrugged now, and smiled over at Lucy. 'I guess my being American put their backs up a little—right?'

'It might have done,' Lucy agreed, 'though one or

two of them seemed to come just to nit-pick. They aren't prepared to give the scheme a chance!'

'It's early days yet, little Lucy, so don't despair,' Joe put in, and Lucy winced. It was the first time he had called her that in front of anyone else, and she saw the startled expression that flashed across Harry's face. 'We've given them food for thought, and that's the main thing,' he went on easily.

'It seems so unfair, though. Just because we haven't any data to give them, any guarantee that the idea will work, they're prepared to condemn it out of hand! Surely they——' Lucy hurried on, warming to her task, but Joe's chuckle stopped her in mid-sentence.

'Don't get carried away, Lucy! They'll come round to our way of thinking sooner or later.' Sister Shepham had already gone off duty, and Joe glanced at his watch, frowning a little. 'I had a shock when I saw the time,' he admitted, then smiled at them both. 'How about the two of you joining me for a bite to eat at that new place in the High Street?'

Harry grinned at him, but Lucy hesitated, then reluctantly shook her head. 'I'm sorry, but I've got one or two chores to do at home, so I'll be getting along now.' She hoped that Joe might try to detain her, but he didn't, merely shrugged.

She heard him and Harry agreeing to meet later for a meal, then the door closed behind her, and she made her way to the car, wishing, after all, that she had accepted his invitation. Surely with Harry there she would have been safe from Joe's charm?

'Staff Nurse! Might I have a word?' The man in question stood on the doorstep of the unit, and a reluctant Lucy turned and retraced her steps.

'Yes, Professor?' she said politely when she came up to him. Joe didn't speak, but there was no need for words between them.

'Won't you join us later, Lucy?' he said at last, but she shook her head. Stubborn he might think her, but there was still too much between them.

'I think,' she began carefully, 'that I spend quite enough time with you, Professor Kingsley. I do need *some* off duty—I actually have a life away from the hospital, you know,' she went on brightly. 'Tomorrow I'm being wined and dined by Dr Asher, so tonight I have to stay in and wash my hair,' she added. It was a stupid remark, but all the clever phrases she thought of to use against him went out of her head once they were actually together. She had no other weapons—and what use were words against that near-fatal charm?

Joe's smile was lopsided, but he didn't seem at all put out by her blunt speaking. 'That's it, little Lucy, put me in my place,' he said very softly, and she flinched.

'I—I didn't mean it that way, Joe,' she whispered. 'But you will——'

'At least you called me Joe,' he commented, then put out a hand and gently touched her cheek. 'Be good, little Lucy.'

Then he walked away from her, towards his own car, leaving a stunned and miserable Lucy standing there.

Lucy gazed at David in dismay, her lunch untouched in front of her. 'Oh, David, you can't mean it! You don't need to leave the Weston General yet, surely?'

David nodded glumly, staring down at his plate. 'I do, if I'm to get the sort of post I want. Being junior registrar to old Geordie Joe is no fun, believe me! I've got another two months to go, then I'm off, perhaps to the bright lights of London town!' He glanced up quickly, then smiled at her stunned expression. 'Miss me, will you?'

'Of course I will! Anyway, it isn't for a little while yet,' Lucy said quietly. 'The professor isn't that difficult to get on with, is he? He's a bit of a slave-driver, I know, but——'

'That, dearest Lucy, is the understatement of the year! I'm not afraid of hard work, as you know, but he——'

'Neither is he,' Lucy put in quickly. 'For every hour you work, he probably works two,' she defended, then wished she hadn't, as David's eyes narrowed.

'I see how the land lies,' was all he said, but Lucy wanted to hurl something at him.

'I can't pretend that I don't know what you mean, but it isn't like that at all. Just because I knew Joe before, it doesn't mean I'm blind to his faults.'

'It's Joe now, is it? You were always careful to call him the professor until I found out about your— previous relationship with him.'

Lucy gasped, the slight hesitation in David's speech being all too obvious. 'That isn't fair! Anyway, it's all in the past now,' she insisted, but David shook his head, a lock of hair falling across his eye.

'Since I'm paying so much for this plate of chicken perhaps we'd better eat some,' he suggested, apparently closing his ears to Lucy's remarks, but she shook her head, before pushing the plate to one side.

'I'll just have coffee, thank you, or perhaps an ice-cream. Don't worry,' she hurried on, as David appeared about to argue, 'I'll pay my share. That's the least I can do.'

'Yes, I suppose it is,' he agreed, tucking into his own meal with apparent enthusiasm. 'Anyway, I wanted you to know that I'll be leaving the hospital. I've got one or two jobs in mind. The thing is, though——' he hesitated, tugging at his earlobe, then grimacing '—I need a reference from the old man. Well, of course I'll get one anyway, but you couldn't find out how he feels about me, I suppose?' he rushed on.

'How am I supposed to go about that?' Lucy asked with interest. 'He doesn't discuss you or any of the other doctors, and I can hardly stick my nose in. He'll wonder.'

'No, he won't. He must know we're, well, good friends. He's seen us together, surely? Anyway, he knew we were lunching together today. You told him, I suppose?' His bland blue gaze met hers.

'Well, yes, I did, as a matter of fact,' Lucy admitted, remembering the previous afternoon—remembering too, what she had said to Joe. Her eyes darkened with a sadness she didn't understand. The man had a hide like a rhino's, and her words were simply so many paper darts bouncing off the rhino's hide, but she needn't have, *shouldn't* have said them.

'Still with me, are you, Lucy?' David's tone was astringent.

Sadly Lucy gazed across at him. 'Yes, still here. I—I—what did he say about it?'

'I was put out for a bit, because I thought he was going to tell me I couldn't have the afternoon off, though heaven knows I'm owed this, and more! But he was as nice as pie about it, told me to go early as well, so I took an extra hour,' David explained, and it was Lucy's turn to raise her brow.

'Extraordinary,' she murmured. 'If you don't want to stay for a pudding, we——'

'No, no, I'm just finished,' David said. 'There, we'll have that ice-cream you wanted, and no, you can't pay your share,' he added firmly. 'Sharon wants us to have a meal with her some time next week. Barry's away and she's at a loose end. She's got an old friend staying with her, and she's instructed me to find a bloke for the friend, then there'll be us two, and——'

David went on happily planning a meal Lucy had no intention of going to, and she blanked out his voice, wishing she were dining at Joe's house instead.

'Sharon says if there's anyone else you want to bring, the more the merrier! We'll have a bit of a party, shall we? Oh, and bring a bottle. No, I'll bring a bottle, and you could make something, couldn't you?' David was saying, and Lucy brought her mind back to the mundane things of life.

Joe's lazy smile and deep-set eyes faded from her mind, and she sighed. 'How about Dr Harry? She must be lonely so far from her home—though I suppose she's too old. She won't fit in with Sharon's friends.'

David looked surprised but agreed readily enough to invite her. 'What about your stepsister? Would she like to join us?

'I was just about to mention her. I know she'd love a party. I've promised to look about for some in the nurses' home but they mightn't appreciate another girl coming in from outside. Never mind, she'll enjoy Sharon's party. And I'll see Dr Harry tomorrow,' Lucy promised.

She was nearly ten minutes late getting back to the unit, but, like David, she was owed time—quite a lot of it.

Another person who was owed time by the hospital was Joe Kingsley himself, and he was sitting at his desk as she passed his office. She paused only briefly, but long enough to see that he had a packet of sandwiches in front of him and a flask. Another working lunch. Sad because she couldn't relieve his work load, Lucy was busily reworking her schedule of patients a few minutes later when he appeared in the doorway. She glanced up warily, wondering what was coming. Somehow she summoned up a smile, and Joe chuckled, the sound warming her.

'Think I was going to tick you off for being, now, let me see——' he paused to consult his watch '—for being approximately eight minutes late back from lunch. Did you enjoy your meal?' He came right into the office, and to Lucy's dismay turned the office chair the wrong way round and sat facing her, resting his chin on the chair's back, his eyes, dark, unfathomable pools.

'I'm very sorry about the eight minutes, Professor,' she murmured dutifully, and his eyes glinted with amusement. 'I wish——' she said, then stopped. What she had been about to say was that she wished he would go back to his own room and leave her to get on. His was too disturbing a presence for her to concentrate on what she was doing.

'Yes? You wish—what?' he prompted, and, irritated, Lucy shrugged.

'Nothing; it doesn't matter. Oh, is Dr Harry about? No, it's her afternoon off, isn't it? David's sister is throwing a party some time next week and he said I could invite Harry—do you think she would come?' Lucy met Joe's eyes reluctantly, glad that she had found a safe topic of conversation.

'She might—Harry loves parties,' Joe went on, a little smile crossing his face. 'As a matter of fact, I'm taking her to one tonight, so. . .' He rose and smiled down at Lucy, that lazy smile she had grown to mistrust, the smile that held all the promise of a hot summer evening.

'I hope you both enjoy your evening,' Lucy said woodenly, then quickly bent her head to her work, so that Joe shouldn't see the hurt in her eyes. Anyway, what did it matter to her that Joe was seeing Harry Hamilton socially? It ought not to matter.

'Lucy?'

Startled, Lucy glanced up. 'Oh, you're still here!'

Joe gazed down at her thoughtfully for a moment, then turned away without another word. Lucy heard his footsteps retreating along the corridor. It was a lonely sound, somehow, and she couldn't bear it—Joe was walking away from her. Without conscious thought she hurried after him, and got to his door just as he was about to close it. Now that she was here Lucy didn't know what to say, didn't know how to excuse her strange behaviour.

'Yes, Lucy?' There was a wry smile on Joe's face. 'Was there something you wanted to tell me?'

Lucy opened her mouth, but before she could speak he was urging her into his office and closing the door with a snap behind them. Then he let go of her arm and stood, arms folded, leaning against the door.

'All right, I'll make it easier for you,' he said.

'There's still too much between us; we both remember the past all too vividly. But there isn't anything either of us can do about that, little Lucy.'

'Yes, you're right, of course. It's stupid trying to ignore the past, though, trying to pretend it never happened,' Lucy said slowly. She *had* tried to forget, had pushed it to the back of her mind, but there was no doubt that Joe was right—their previous relationship coloured their view of each other now. She raised her eyes to his in a look of such mute pleading that Joe groaned softly. His arms were no longer folded; he had dropped them to his side, and Lucy's glance went to his hands, which he was clenching and unclenching as he fought for control.

She knew then that the future, *their* future lay in her bidding. If she made a move towards him now, Joe's arms would open wide and enfold her. If she assured him that the past was dead and that she was almost engaged to David Asher, Joe would accept that. And surely that would be better? Joe didn't love her any more—he had *never* loved her, only desired her, she was sure of it now. If she mentioned her romance with David, that way she would keep her pride intact, even if her heart was shattered into a thousand pieces.

'Perhaps we ought to kiss the past goodbye, Lucy,' Joe said softly, while she agonised over her decision. 'What do you say to that?'

Hastily she back away. 'I don't think that's a good——' she began, then his lips claimed hers, and Lucy quite forgot what she had been about to say.

Wordlessly she clung to him, not protesting even when his lips left hers briefly and trailed a hot, sweet trail down her cheek, her throat, then, as if drawn irresistibly, back to her soft, warm mouth.

When they broke apart Lucy felt bereft, shivery, and longed for Joe's strong arms to encircle her once again. But she wouldn't ask, wouldn't beg, and he showed no inclination to claim her again. Instead, he moved over to the window, head bent. Even from where she stood she could hear his breathing, a harsh, unnatural sound. Yes, Joe had been as moved as she was by the kiss, by the startling realisation that if they had been alone and off duty that kiss might have led to more—much more. They still found each other desirable. Joe still wanted her and she still loved him.

'Was *that* kissing the past goodbye?' she asked breathlessly. Her lips felt swollen where the savagery of Joe's kiss had caught her unawares, and if anyone had come into his office now it would have been obvious that they had been locked in each other's arms only moments before. Thank heaven it was Harriet's afternoon off!

Harry. Yes, she had forgotten Harry—forgotten Rosemary, for that matter. 'I hope you enjoy your evening out, Joe. I've got a few patients to see—I don't expect I'll be back in the unit tonight. Cheerio!' Somehow she injected a hint of lightness into her voice, and even managed to look reasonably cheerful as Joe whirled round.

The agony of mind she herself had endured didn't show in Joe's face, and Lucy's eyes were sad. Perhaps the trauma was all on her side. After all, what was a kiss to a man like that?

'Cheerio, Lucy. Don't work too hard,' he said

blandly, and without another word she opened the
door and forced herself to walk slowly away.

Joe stared at the closed door for a long moment,
before sitting down at his desk and staring blankly at
the work in front of him.

'Tom Noble—did you have any luck with his relatives?'
Harry asked, and reluctantly Lucy shook her head.

'The younger sister ought still to be alive, but I've
heard nothing so far. The trouble is, Mr Noble can't
remember her married name—or he doesn't *want* to
remember,' Lucy added as an afterthought, and Harry
shrugged.

'You could be right,' she agreed, shuffling the case-
notes. 'Now, this Mrs Carlton—can we discharge her
tomorrow?'

'She isn't keen,' Lucy began, and Harry chuckled.
She had a rather dry chuckle which Lucy found
infectious.

'They're never keen,' Harry commented, 'but we
have to draw the line somewhere. Oh, her GP phoned
while you were out. I have a note about him somewhere.' The doctor burrowed into a huge pile of papers
while Lucy looked on, bemused. Harry wasn't all that
tidy but she was efficient in other ways, and the patients
loved her without exception. Well, perhaps there was
one exception—Tom Noble. He rejected any attempts
to help him, and hated the thought of being discharged,
even though he was ready to go out into the
community.

'Yes, here we are. He suggests she's kept in another
couple of days, but I told him we would have to think
about that.'

'Yes,' Lucy said slowly, reluctant to interfere, 'but we have to be careful. I expect Joe mentioned the resistance some GPs are putting up. They feel that sometimes patients are discharged too soon and——'

'Not *our* patients, surely? We're making sure that all the services are alerted and that they go back to at least tolerable home circumstances—that's part of your job,' Dr Harry emphasised. 'You're doing well at it,' she went on with a slow smile. 'Now, I have another couple of patients to see—do you want to come along?'

'Mm, yes, please. Oh—I just remembered. My friend David Asher, well, his sister actually—she's throwing a party next Friday and we thought you might like to come along—would you?'

Harry broke into a delighted smile. 'Why, of course I would—I just love parties! Joe and I were always going to parties and dances when we worked together back home,' she added happily, while Lucy felt anything but happy.

'I'm glad,' she said bleakly. 'Was he—was the professor there long? I know he went to Arabia when he left here; he told me at the interview,' Lucy hurried on, striving to keep a proper balance of interest in her voice, just enough to show that she was curious but not more than that.

'Yes, that's right. I believe he did a year out there— that's where he met my ex-husband,' Harry told her. 'Well, he wasn't an ex then, but he is now! Then Joe spent some time in London.' Harry glanced up, her gaze shrewd. 'You knew Joe before, didn't you?'

'Well, yes, but not very well. So, after London he went out to the States, then?' Lucy hurried on, and Harry nodded.

'You know, I often wondered about that,' the American doctor muttered, almost to herself, 'and now I know. There, that's sorted. Shall we pop into the hospital and see our patients?' She straightened up, her gaze probing.

Lucy wasn't about to give up so easily, though. 'You often wondered about what, Harry?'

'Why Joe left the Weston General—and why he came back,' Harry said obliquely. 'Let's hit the trail!' With an exaggerated gesture she sauntered out, leaving a puzzled Lucy to follow. It was obvious why Joe had left the hospital; he needed to further his career. Why he should come back was another matter, and she busied herself puzzling over it as she caught up with Dr Harry.

The two patients were in men's surgical, but the women found they were interrupting a late ward round so they waited in the sister's office. Then Lucy glanced up in dismay as she heard a familiar voice speaking to the ward sister—it was Joe's round! 'Oh, we've disturbed the professor,' she told Harry, who shrugged.

'I don't disturb the professor; *you* might,' she said with a glint of humour in her grey eyes, and Lucy blushed.

'I keep out of his way as much as possible. I'm sure I'm no bother to him,' she said, deliberately misunderstanding. 'Anyway, he might have something to tell us about those two patients of yours,' she hurried on.

'He just might,' Harry agreed. 'Why don't we ask him?'

The man himself came into the office, frowning. Then his relaxed smile broke out—but the smile was for Harry alone. 'Two of my favourite ladies! You could have come along for the round, Harry.'

'We won't interrupt your session, Joe, but we've called in to see these two.' Harry thrust a couple of folders on to the desk. 'There's Peter Elliott, the splenectomy, and Bert Payne, the patient who had the partial gastrectomy. I thought if it's OK that we could transfer them to Arden tonight, then out into the community in a couple of days. How does that suit you?'

'I'm happy about Mr Payne, if you are, though I suggest he stays on here another day or so. He's got a big family only too happy to have him after that. Peter Elliott's young and fit; he certainly ought to cope, but, given his psychiatric background, he probably won't.'

Peter Elliott, as Joe had surmised, was adamant that he wasn't going home yet. In his case there was a good reason for his reluctance to leave. 'Peter lives in rooms at his sister's and he doesn't think she'll be able to have him home,' Harry told her. Quite a number of their patients lived in lodgings, and Lucy wasn't happy about some of them being discharged early.

Aware that Joe was standing in the ward doorway talking to Sister, Lucy leaned over Peter's bed and smiled warmly at him. 'When do you think you might be ready for discharge, Mr Elliott?'

The patient was only twenty-one, a small young man with sharp features and over-bold blue eyes. 'If you're part of the home nursing team, I'll go straight away!' he laughed, but it was a strained laugh, and clearly he wasn't going to budge if it could be avoided. The accident which had caused the rupture of his spleen had left him with extensive cuts and severe bruising as well as fractured ribs, but he should have been in Arden ward by now, only his psychiatric state preventing his earlier discharge. Peter had been under the care of the psychiatric unit since his early teens because of depression which was quite severe at times. Only Joe's surgical intervention had saved his life, but, according to Harry, the thought that he had nearly died didn't seem to bother him.

'I don't think we need turn you out quite so suddenly, but we thought about transferring you to Arden, our little ward, tonight, and assessing you there. How do you feel about a slight change of scenery?' Lucy asked, her eyes concerned.

Peter shrugged. 'It's my sister—well, the guy she married. She's older than me, bin like a mother she has, but him and me, we don't get on, see? I don't mind coming to your other ward but I ain't——'

'You could be out of hospital in a day or two after that,' Harry interrupted, 'once we've fixed up your home-care nurse. We won't leave you to cope alone.'

Lucy nibbled her lower lip, wishing Harry hadn't mentioned discharge again. This called for a little psychology—clearly the man didn't *want* to be out of hospital in a day or two. The home circumstances needed more investigation.

Nevertheless, Harry was a senior doctor and Lucy couldn't contradict her. She must be brought to see that sometimes a little deviousness wasn't a bad thing. There was a limit to what frankness and a no-nonsense manner could achieve!

'Problems, ladies?' Joe asked, and Lucy felt a stab of irritation. Couldn't he leave them to get on with it?

Surely he trusted Dr Harry even if he thought Staff Nurse Powell was too young and silly to cope?

She rose, struggling to school her mutinous face into some semblance of respect for a consultant, but failing miserably.

Joe's eyes met hers very briefly, and there was a gleam of amusement in their depths. 'Poor little Lucy!' he commented before turning his attention to the patient, leaving Lucy feeling as if she had been kissed.

CHAPTER SIX

LUCY knocked at Joe's office door. It was closed for once and she didn't like to disturb him, but there were Matters To Be Sorted Out, and they couldn't be left any longer. He'd had a heavy morning in theatre, she knew, and——

Abruptly the door opened and Joe stood there, dressed in his executive suit and with a bulging brief-case under his arm. It was a Joe she had never seen before, a grim-faced, hard-eyed stranger, and Lucy took a step back before she could help herself. 'Oh! You're going out, then? I won't——'

'Yes, I do believe I am,' Joe agreed quietly, 'but if you've something important to tell me I can spare you ten minutes. Come in,' he invited, and Lucy took a deep breath and followed him into the office. He might not like what she had to say to him but that wasn't going to stop her from saying it!

'Now, tell me what you're concerned about,' Joe suggested, placing his briefcase in the corner and unbuttoning his jacket. He looked tired, Lucy thought in dismay. No, more than that; unutterably weary.

There were a lot of things she was concerned about, and one of them was Joe, but patients came first. 'Peter Elliott,' she began. 'He isn't ready for discharge yet— at least *he* doesn't think so, and I wondered if he could be allowed to stay a little longer?'

As promised, they had moved him to Arden, and

Lucy had managed to persuade Harry not to discharge him, home-care team or no home-care team, but the ward was full now and there seemed no alternative to letting him return to what Lucy considered to be inadequate home circumstances. True, the flat he shared with his sister was in a modern block and wasn't the slum dwelling Peter had led her to expect, but from Peter's point of view it was far from ideal. He wasn't, though, the sort of person who could survive alone and there seemed no question of his leaving his sister and brother-in-law in peace and moving elsewhere.

'He *has* been allowed to stay a little longer, Lucy, but I'm afraid his time's up; he'll have to go home tomorrow at the latest. Preferably today,' Joe said firmly, but Lucy wasn't going to let go without an argument.

'I know he's young and just the sort of patient you want for the home-care scheme, but he lodges with his sister. It's three flights up and once the home-care nurses stop visiting he'll be——'

'Fit to resume light duties at work,' Joe finished for her. 'The man isn't an invalid, Lucy. Be reasonable. He's the type of patient we want for the home-care— you've just admitted as much yourself,' he said, gently chiding, and Lucy agreed that she had.

'But he isn't——'

'What alternative is there? You tell me,' Joe invited, leaning towards her slightly, a quiet smile on his face, and Lucy swallowed. She mistrusted him in this equable mood, but plunged on regardless.

Somehow she found herself telling him about her dream of a convalescent home, a halfway house where patients not suitable for discharge could begin their convalescence. 'It's just the sort of scheme made for people like Peter,' she enthused, her eyes alight, but Joe's expression was so tender, his smile so warm that she faltered. When he was in this mood he was totally irresistible. 'I'm sorry; I shouldn't have gone on like that. And I do understand about your needing the bed. Would you like me to see him now? Or will Harry tell him he's to be discharged?'

'I rather think she's seeing to that. She mentioned your belief that he ought to stay longer, but we can't make exceptions, Lucy; you must see that. If the scheme is to work at all we have to make rules—and stick to them,' Joe warned. Then he turned aside to picked up his briefcase, watched miserably by Lucy. 'Sometimes I wonder whether the scheme *will* work with so many staff against it,' he commented, frowning a little, and Lucy longed to ease away the worry lines.

Then she remembered, just in time. Let Dr Harry or his wife do that. She was just little Staff Nurse Powell. Once before she had given in to the urge to comfort him, and look where it had got her!

'Your face lost its brightness just then, Lucy,' Joe commented, hugging his briefcase to him. It was a curiously defensive gesture and made him seem vulnerable, lost, perhaps a little unsure of himself—something Joe Kingsley had never been.

'I—Joe, what's the matter? Can't you tell me? No, I suppose you can't,' Lucy went on painfully, suspecting that it was some domestic upset again. She had no right to ask and certainly didn't want his thinking she was being inquisitive.

'We lost a patient this morning, Lucy. No, *I* lost a patient; it was my decision to operate,' Joe said, half to himself, wondering still if it had been the right decision. If he had been offered the same choice again he wasn't sure if he would have chosen surgery, but he would never know.

Lucy was stunned, her big blue eyes full of love and sympathy for him. Her lips parted, and she was aware of Joe's sharp intake of breath before he abruptly strode from the room without even saying goodbye. She was left alone in the office, staring at the door, her heart so full that she couldn't have spoken even if Joe *had* returned.

Before she could collect herself the door opened again and she tensed. 'Oh, it's you, Harry! Did you want the professor? He's just left,' Lucy hurried on, trying to ignore the strange look Harry gave her.

'Yes, I just talked to him. I didn't know you were in here,' the doctor commented, beginning to search through Joe's desk. 'There's a report here somewhere, about a home-care scheme that's already operating down south. Have you seen it, Lucy?'

'Mm? No, at least I *have*, but not in Joe—in Professor Kingsley's desk. Sister has it now, I think. Harry—who died?' she blurted out, and Harry's probing gaze rested on her for a moment.

'You know about that? Joe hasn't talked to any of us about it. It was a patient on Hathaway, a Mrs Peterson. She'd been in before, and——'

'Mrs Peterson! I know her! I knew her,' Lucy hastily amended. 'She was a favourite of mine, so keen to hear all the news about the nurses, so pleased when I got the job here. She was discharged but I didn't think she would be back so soon,' she went on painfully. Poor Mrs Peterson.

'Snap out of it, Lucy! We can't win 'em all! Surgeons have to keep a certain distance from their patients, but I guess you know that. We mustn't get too involved with them, but sometimes Joe does,' Harry admitted, and Lucy silently echoed that.

'I'll go and get that report for you,' she said wanly. She made her escape, needing to be alone, wondering if Joe, too, needed to be alone.

As she had promised, Lucy saw Peter Elliott safely out of hospital and back home to his sister's flat not far from the centre of town.

When she had called there before speaking to Joe about it, she had been astonished to find such a modern block. Young Peter probably hadn't meant to mislead her, but she had assumed, from what he had said, that the building was falling apart at the seams. There were family problems, though, which would make his mental condition worse, and Lucy still wasn't happy. She had visions of his being turned out on the street sooner rather than later, but knew the problem wasn't hers. As with Carol Barrett, there was little the home-care scheme could do other than see him safely home and provide what little district nursing care might be needed.

'Welcome home, Nurse Lucy,' Peter said as the ambulance stopped outside, then rushed on. 'You're probably thinking how awful it looks, but——'

'No, I wasn't,' Lucy broke in quickly. 'From what you said, I had imagined a rather older building. A bit worn at the edges, shall we say?' she went on, and Peter had the grace to look uncomfortable, but only momentarily. He had to let them into the flat since his sister was nowhere in evidence.

'There won't be anyone to see I'm all right,' he whined.

'I'll see you're all right, Peter, don't worry,' Lucy spoke soothingly, not wanting to agitate him. 'Male Nurse Atkins is coming along later and he'll see you settled in. You can talk to him; he's nice.'

Peter continued to grumble, but, after she had sorted out his belongings, Lucy went to put the kettle on. Peter's sister had told her to make herself at home when she brought Peter back. She was just setting out biscuits on a plate when she heard voices coming from the sitting-room. Then Peter's much older sister appeared in the kitchen doorway, carrying a big shopping-bag and looking harassed.

Lucy turned to her with a smile. 'Just in time for tea! I hope you don't mind my taking over your kitchen?'

'No, I'm glad to have someone make me a cup of tea!' the woman admitted, dumping her shopping on the floor. 'Weighs a ton, this does!' Fanning herself, she flopped down on a chair. 'I see his lordship's back, then,' she commented, taking the cup of tea Lucy handed her.

'Yes, we've finally discharged him. He——' Lucy hesitated, not wanting to offend the woman. 'He seems to think he won't be able to manage, but the male nurse—Nurse Atkins—will be here shortly, and we wouldn't have discharged your brother if we hadn't made adequate nursing arrangments.'

'No, I don't suppose you would, but Peter gets depressed, you know. He enjoyed the company up at the hospital. My husband will be in tonight, but him and Peter don't get on and I'm the one caught in the middle,' the woman said. 'Still, I expect you've got problems enough of your own, eh?'

'Nurses don't have problems. Nor do doctors.' Lucy smiled. 'At least, we're supposed to keep them hidden during duty hours! Is there anything else I can do for you? I'm not in a hurry to get back.'

'No, I'll just finish my tea then sort young Peter out. Then it'll be time to put my old man's dinner on. I'll be all right, dear,' she assured Lucy.

Reluctanly, Lucy left. Three flights of stairs later, she was out in the busy street. She eventually found a zebra crossing, and as she stepped off the pavement she caught sight of a car that was only too familiar: Joe Kingsley's Jaguar.

She couldn't imagine what he was doing in the neighbourhood, but smiled her thanks as she crossed over, then went in search of a bus to take her back to the unit. It would have been nice if Joe had been on his way back and could have given her a lift, but after all the trauma Lucy felt it better not to ask. Anyway, he had a passenger—a blonde she didn't recognise, but she had the awful feeling it was Rosemary Kingsley.

Joe wasn't at the Weston when she got back and, according to Edna Shepham, he was off duty. Since the death of Mrs Peterson, Lucy hadn't had the chance to really talk to him. Perhaps, as Harry had said, he kept a certain distance from patients and wasn't as upset about it as she would have been, yet he must be shaken, surely? He must need a little tender loving care—and Staff Nurse Lucy Powell was only too willing to offer him some!

'Did you want him for anything in particular, Lucy?' Edna went on. 'I'm seeing him tonight—I could give him a message, if you like,' she offered, but Lucy quickly shook her head.

Edna was seeing him tonight! He certainly believed in playing the field, Lucy thought unfairly as she drove home some time later. His wife was still in evidence, then there was Edna, not to mention Dr Harry. Young Sadie, too, seemed smitten by him, and Lucy recalled seeing him lunching with a staff nurse from one of the surgical wards recently. He certainly didn't need any tender loving care from *her*! Her lips curved into a sad smile. She wished desperately she could be the one to offer a shoulder to cry on, but as long as Joe had someone that was what mattered.

'Ah, there you are, Lucy.' Joe's voice was unexpectedly warm, and Lucy glanced up warily. She was in the Arden ward office a few days later, writing up the notes for one of their new patients, since Edna Shepham had gone off sick earlier that day.

'Yes, here I am,' she agreed, then the telephone shrilled and she reached out automatically to answer it. Unfortunately so did Joe, and their hands met on the receiver before Lucy snatched hers away, feeling as if she had been touched by a red-hot iron. Hastily she buried herself in the case-notes while Joe tended to the caller. When he replaced the receiver, she was busily writing again and she didn't glance up.

'Since Edna Shepham is going to be off sick for at least a couple of days, please consider yourself acting ward sister,' he said, surprising her. 'Until Friday, anyway. Her wisdom tooth's bothering her so much she's going to have it extracted,' he added.

'She's been in pain for quite a while,' Lucy commented, 'but she's so keen on her new job she didn't want to take time off!'

'Never mind, while we have Staff Nurse Powell we're fine,' Joe said, and Lucy gazed at him suspiciously, not sure whether she was meant to laugh at the joke. He could hardly be serious!

'Whatever you say,' she agreed. 'Naturally, you're lucky to have me here,' she continued, 'but I can't do both jobs, even for two days.' She glanced up expectantly, surprising that tender expression on Joe's face again.

Right now she needed someone to feel tender towards her, what with alarums and excursions at home, with her father getting uptight because her mother wasn't coming down just yet, and Sadie getting all the praise for whatever Lucy herself did.

'I've taken care of all that—Staff Nurse Baynes is being seconded for the rest of the week, and heaven help you if she isn't as efficient as you keep assuring me she is!'

'Heather's coming to Arden?' Lucy brightened up immediately. 'Thank you! She really is efficient; you'll be surprised.

'I'll be amazed,' Joe said drily, 'but never mind. At least I've lifted the gloom from your shoulders. Your little face was beginning to look quite pinched,' he went on.

'Was it? Oh, I'm sorry, but I've got a lot on my mind,' Lucy hurried on, not wanting him to know *why* her face had been looking pinched! 'My father's a bit put out because Mum isn't coming down to see him after all, but he's got Sadie—he ought to be happy,' she muttered, half to herself, then settled down to her work again. It wasn't any business of Joe's and he wouldn't be interested, anyway.

'Cheer up, little Lucy. How about a nice tour of the Shakespeare hotspots one day soon? Edna should be back, and I can arrange some cover for the ward if we choose a day when we've no one being discharged.

'Shakespeare's hotspots? Do you mean all the tourist attractions?'

'I expect you've seen them, but I haven't, not all of them anyway. How about it?' He settled himself on one corner of the desk, his gaze searching, and Lucy couldn't look away.

'Well, I've never bothered much about Shakespeare, to tell you the truth,' she admitted, her voice shaky. It was difficult not to glance away, but she was determined not to let him know how much his presence disturbed her. 'I've been to the theatre, of course, several times. Oh, and I've seen Anne Hathaway's cottage, but I think that's all. When you live in the area you don't always bother sightseeing—you know they'll be there whenever you want them! But I'd like to see them very much. Thank you,' she added politely, but Joe's lazy chuckle nearly unnerved her, and she wasn't quick enough to disguise the longing in her eyes.

'Perhaps we ought to invite Harry as well?' Joe suggested, uneasily aware that Lucy might read too much into the invitation. He wanted to spend the day with her as much as she obviously did with him, but he was being a fool and knew it. There was safety in numbers—damn it, he didn't *want* to include Harry in the invitation!

'Yes, she would like that,' Lucy said coolly. She

hated the idea of sharing her day out with Dr Harry, but it would, she conceded, be for the best—there was safety in numbers.

'Would your stepsister like to come? She might be interested in meeting Harry,' Joe suggested, thinking that Sadie and Harry could pair up while he wandered around with his little Lucy.

Lucy's temper flared. 'I don't know why you don't close the unit and take *all* the staff out for the day! If Harry, why not Heather? And if Sadie, why not my father? Then there's Edna Shepham—don't forget her!' Lucy was aware that she was behaving badly, aware, too, of Joe's astonished gaze. It wouldn't be many seconds before he lost his temper, but she couldn't stop herself. A dam had burst and there was no stopping the forces of nature. 'And why not your wife and—and——' she searched her mind wildly for the name of the staff nurse she had seen him with '—oh, yes, Nurse Marsh!' She gulped down with a sob, shaking with anger and temper. Even if he was to dismiss her on the spot, she wouldn't apologise, she wouldn't!

'Nurse Marsh?' Joe echoed, perplexed. He wasn't sure what he had done to spark off the display of temper, but he knew one thing—Lucy was irresistible when she was in a rage! He began to laugh softly, which incensed Lucy still further. She would *not* be laughed at!

'I'm glad I—I've amused you,' she said brokenly, getting to her feet and glaring at him. Since she came only to his shoulder, this wasn't easy, and she was forced to tilt her head up to meet his amused gaze. 'I don't think I want to tramp around a lot of stuffy old houses, thank you very much, but I'm sure Sadie would be delighted. She likes you,' she went on, uneasily aware that she was making matters worse.

'Does she?' Joe's voice was hollow. 'Another teen-age conquest,' he said bitterly, and Lucy flushed.

'Yes, that's right! Another young girl falling victim to the older man's charismatic charm!'

'Am I charming and charismatic? Thank you, Lucy,' Joe said, white teeth gleaming in a smile that she considered wolfish. 'You wouldn't be jealous, by any chance, would you? No, of course you wouldn't. After all, you told me the past was dead, didn't you?

Joe still seemed amused, and Lucy knew she ought to apologise, get them back on their usual easy footing, but she couldn't, she wouldn't!

'About Rosemary,' he began. 'She's——' Then the telephoned shrilled again, and this time he made no attempt to answer it. Lucy deliberately turned her back on him, but the query was easily dealt with, and she reluctantly replaced the receiver, knowing she must say sorry, no matter what it cost.

Joe was still there, his eyes sad, making him all the more appealing. 'Joe,' she began softly, 'I'm sorry for what I said. I shouldn't have said it,' she finished stiffly, annoyed because he wasn't helping her out.

'Shouldn't have said what, Lucy? That remark about my charismatic charm could be construed as a compliment, I suppose,' he commented, a rueful expression on his face.

'It wasn't meant that way, but you *are* charming, when you want to be,' Lucy qualified. 'Sadie does like you, though. That wasn't meant unkindly, but. . .' Her voice trailed off, and Joe finished the sentence for her.

'But you rather wish she didn't, beause she reminds you of yourself as a teenager, falling head over heels in love with Joe Kingsley—then finding out, too late, that he was married,' Joe said, his voice taut.

Lucy nodded, averting her gaze, then realised that she had admitted to falling in love with him. No! She wouldn't give him that satisfaction; she had her pride if she had nothing else! 'No, not quite like that. *I* didn't fall head over heels in love with you, as you put it, but Sadie might. She's very impressionable.'

'And you weren't?'

'I have to admit I was taken with you, yes,' Lucy admitted, 'but I certainly didn't fall in *love* with you. It was purely physical,' she averred, hoping he wouldn't probe too deeply.

'Was it?' Joe's tone was bleak, and Lucy flinched. 'Yes, I suppose it was. Physical on both our parts. You were excellent in bed, Lucy, and so, I'm told, am I. It's a pity we can't pick up where we left off, but there's nothing deader than the ashes of an old fire, is there?'

With that parting shot he left, closing the door sharply behind him. Lucy just stared into space, knowing that Joe was right—nothing could breathe life back into yesterday's fire.

CHAPTER SEVEN

'ARE you sure Sharon won't mind?' Lucy asked as David parked rather haphazardly in front of his sister's house on the evening of the party.

'Mind about what, love? Surely all those cars can't be at the party? There's hundreds!'

'That's what I mean. Sharon seems to have enough guests for a dozen parties already. Will she mind us bringing two more—she probably hasn't catered for so many?' Knowing Sharon, she probably hadn't catered for *any*, but Lucy refrained from saying so. She could see herself spending the next hour or two in the kitchen hastily making sandwiches. It was a good job she had thought to bring a few rations, despite David's insistence that she was bringing far too much.

The car carrying Dr Harry and Sadie swung alongside them, and David wound down his window and waved cheerily. 'Glad we didn't lose you! I think you'll have to park in Northbourne Road—it's just at the back there. Come on, Lucy, let's get that food inside. Lord, you've brought enough to feed Napoleon's army!' he commented, taking one of the heavy bags from her and leading the way to the open front door, from which loud music was already coming.

Sharon greeted them enthusiastically, and when Lucy saw her hostess's party dress of filmy gauze she was glad she had chosen to dress up. Sadie had decided to wear the pretty green and gold outfit and had pressed

116

Lucy to borrow whatever she wished. Since Sadie was so much bigger, that was rather a problem, but eventually Lucy had settled upon a cream silk blouse of her own teamed with a black moiré skirt belonging to Sadie, who had obligingly tacked it up so that it wasn't too long. Sadie was also wearing the pearl brooch that properly belonged to Lucy, but in exchange had lent her several strands of gold chain. Mr Powell had pronounced them both to be belles of the ball, and Lucy felt happier than she had done for days. She was determined to put Joe Kingsley right out of her mind and thoroughly enjoy herself, entering into the spirit of the party, even if she *did* have to spend half the evening making sandwiches!

She waited in the entrance for the arrival of Sadie and Harry, then let out a gasp when she saw the American doctor's dress—what she had termed her 'formal'. With her glowing red hair, the colour Harry had chosen was just right, corn-gold figured silk with a high neck and a pie-crust collar, the lines of the dress making the most of her very slender figure.

'Oh, Harry, you look lovely!'

'Thank you, Lucy—I hope Prince Charming likes it, too!' she laughed, but before Lucy could ask whom she meant Harry and Sadie had been enveloped in Sharon's embrace and taken in tow, while Lucy herself made for the kitchen where David was already ensconced, putting the wine and beer away.

'Looks like we're on kitchen duty. Still, we can have our own private party in here, can't we?' he laughed, giving her a squeeze that took Lucy's breath away. Anxious not to spoil the evening, she allowed herself to be kissed. To her relief it was a tepid kiss, David's mind clearly being elsewhere. A little later she found out what was on his mind. As she might have guessed, it was their mutual boss.

'Do you know what that man's done?' he demanded as she prepared to carry in a platter of canapés.

'Who? Professor Kinglsey?' she asked without interest, and David shot her a sharp look.

'Yes, Professor Kingsley—your Joe.'

'He is not my Joe!' Lucy flared, almost upsetting the canapés. David was only just in time to catch the plate, and an annoyed Lucy swept out of the kitchen before he could say more. Her Joe, indeed!

When she saw the guest being greeted by both Sharon and Dr Harry, she nearly dropped the plate for the second time. It was Joe Kingsley! His eyes met hers, and he smiled lazily. 'Hello, Lucy. Busy?'

Sharon laughed. 'Lucy's a great help. Without her and David on kitchen duty I don't know how I'd manage! Oh, and Sadie's going to help, as well,' she added, as Sadie pushed her way through the throng and headed towards the kitchen.

'Perhaps I'd better lend a hand since I'm a gate-crasher,' Joe said, neatly removing the plate from Lucy's suddenly nerveless fingers and offering it around, after taking one of the goodies and handing it to Lucy, who stared down at it numbly.

'Eat up, little Lucy; don't let good food go to waste,' Joe urged, and she did as she was bid, wondering what malevolent goblin had sent Joe there this evening.

'I didn't know you were coming,' she said, when he returned to her, the plate empty.

'If you had known, would you have come?' he challenged, and Lucy began to shake her head, then stopped. Why give him the satisfaction of knowing that?

'It wouldn't have made any difference to me,' she said, striving to sound nonchalant, but, judging by the gleam of amusement in his eyes, failing miserably. 'No, it wouldn't!' she insisted, and Joe shrugged before passing by on his way to the kitchen.

The music had got louder, and when someone grabbed her, swinging her into a dance, Lucy didn't protest. She wasn't in any hurry to go back to the kitchen—let Sadie entertain him!

'Friend of David's, are you?' her partner bellowed in her ear, and Lucy nodded and smiled, not thinking it worthwhile to raise her voice. 'His girlfriend isn't here tonight, then,' the tall, reedy young man went on, his glance admiring as it rested upon Lucy's flushed face.

'Isn't she?' Lucy asked in dismay as the music stopped momentarily and her partner relinquished her hand. 'I rather thought she was.'

'No, haven't seen her—with hair like that she'd stand out a mile! Lucky guy! I'll get you a drink—there's a guy around here with a tray somewhere. Don't go away!' The reedy young man disappeared into the crush, and Lucy made her way to the kitchen, her mind numb, her feet moving automatically. With hair like that she'd stand out a mile! *Who* would? She began to search her mind for a nurse with hair of a startling colour but could come up with no one. It was ridiculous, anyway; that man had confused David with someone else.

'Lucy?' Joe's kind eyes smiled down into hers, and

Lucy thought she had never been so glad to see him in her life.

'I'm being pursued by a man who wants to offer me a drink—I thought I'd hide in the kitchen!' she said breathlessly, but Joe's eyes narrowed. Something had upset Lucy and he would have taken bets it wasn't because someone had tried to monopolise her.

He looked around for somewhere to put the tray of drinks, then finally left it beside the big rubber plant which was stuck in one corner of the room. Then, taking Lucy's arm firmly, he led her past the kitchen, through the side-door and out into the garden. It was a pleasant evening and already couples were strolling hand in hand, and he and Lucy went unremarked.

'If you're not enjoying the party, we could slip away,' Joe offered, and Lucy tensed.

'No, thank you. I came with—with David and I ought to leave with him. That's only fair,' she said firmly. But was David playing fair with her? If only she hadn't danced with that officious man!

'Lucy? Is there something on your mind? I'd like to kiss away those tears you're desperate to let fall, but right now isn't the time or the place,' Joe said bluntly, and Lucy caught her breath. There was a tight pain in her chest and Joe's words caused her more pain, more anguish.

'It's nothing. I had rather a surprise, that's all.' That, at least, was no lie. 'I've got a headache coming—I wish someone would turn the music down—or, better still, throw the whole lot out of the window!' she said with feeling, and Joe chuckled.

'That's what I was thinking, but I put it down to old

age. I'm getting a bit too long in the tooth for this kind of party, but Harry wanted me to come, so here I am.'

Lucy wanted to cry out with the mental pain, the sorrow. Joe's remark, funnily enough, hurt her more than being told that David had another girlfriend. It cut her like a knife and she couldn't think straight for a moment. Then pride came to her rescue. 'I hope you haven't lost her—I haven't seen her for quite a while. I'd better get back to the kitchen. Thank you for rescuing me,' she added as an afterthought, then hurried into the kitchen, where she found Sadie and Harry busily cutting sausage rolls in half.

'Hi! We missed you,' Harry said. 'There isn't enough food to go around so——'

'We're chopping everything in half!' Sadie interrupted, and both of them went off into gales of laughter. Clearly Harry was enjoying herself and Lucy couldn't find it in her heart to be jealous of the woman.

When at length David turned up, Lucy eyed him warily. Of course she wouldn't say anything to him. After all, what credence could she place on her dancing partner's words? It was better just to pretend nothing had happened, and see what David had to say for himself. He dropped a light kiss on her brow, then grinned, obviously happy, and Lucy realised she had been worrying unnecessarily.

'Sorry I've been missing, but I met a chap I haven't seen for months. Don't know where Sharon got hold of him. Anyway, here I am in all my glory!' He glanced around quickly then caught Lucy to him and planted a kiss full of her mouth. Startled for a moment, she attempted to pull away, then remembered that this was David, not Joe or some drunken stranger.

David held her apart for a moment, his gaze puzzled. 'Sorry, did I take you by surprise?'

'Yes, you did rather! You neglect me all evening, then the minute you turn up you start kissing me! What's a girl to think?' She put laughter into her voice, but David clearly didn't think it was funny.

'That's me put in my place,' he said quietly. 'Oh, by the way, I was telling you about the old man, wasn't I? Did you know he was coming tonight? I suppose you did,' he went on morosely.

'Of course I didn't! I don't know what he does in his off-duty moments! Harry asked him to come, or so he told me,' she said defensively.

'So *that's* how the land lies, is it? Well, they're both about forty, aren't they? Come and meet this guy I was telling you about.' He took Lucy's arm, urging her forward, but she protested. She had the awful feeling that 'this guy' was going to be the young man she had been dancing with!

'No, I won't come now, thank you. Sadie needs a hand with the food, and you know what Sharon's like. She——'

'No, what *is* she like? I thought you enjoyed Sharon's parties,' David said huffily. 'Anyway, I'll give you a hand in the kitchen. Most of the food's gone now, anyway. Never mind, as long as there's plenty to drink.'

And there was, Lucy thought. If Sharon had stinted on the food, she hadn't done so on the alcohol, and already one or two guests were a little under the influence. David's friend was one of them, she realised a few minutes later as he weaved his way towards her. David had disappeared again, and she was temporarily alone in the kitchen, though Harry was within call as she took a breath of fresh air—without Joe, Lucy was glad to note. In fact, Joe seemed to have left the party, though, stuck as she was in the kitchen, she couldn't be sure who was there and who wasn't.

'Ah, there you are!' The kitchen door crashed back and her erstwhile dancing partner beamed at her.

'Yes, here I am! Stuck on permanent kitchen duty, I'm afraid. Here. . .' Lucy thrust a plate of minute sandwiches at him. 'This is the last, so I've cut them up small. Would you take them around for me? It's very sweet of you to offer,' she hurried on, as he gazed blankly down at the plate, clearly not able to focus properly.

'Take them around? Oh, you mean into the party? No, I'd rather take you around. Here's a drink for you—I keep getting you one and having to drink it myself because you've disappeared!' he burbled happily, and Lucy went forward to take the glass. It was always better to humour people who were a bit tipsy.

'Thanks. What is it?' she asked, then her companion's long arms wound themselves around her slender body. Before she could open her mouth to scream, his lips had descended on hers, and she was forced to suffer the indignity of being kissed by someone who reeked of drink, sweat and, in additon, suffered from halitosis!

The moment he freed her she screamed, and Harry came running in, already pushing back the sleeves of her long gown, apparently intending to give a boxing demonstration. The man took one look at Harry, then lumbered towards her. 'Hello! I haven't seen you before. Would *you* like a drink? No one else wants it.' He held out the glass, from which most of the fluid had spilled, but Harry pushed him away and, in falling, he fell against Lucy, who couldn't get out of the way in time.

In the uproar no one noticed Joe appear from the direction of the garden. His bemused gaze took in Lucy sprawled on the floor, with a thin young man lying half across her, and Harry, with her sleeves rolled up, trying to half tug, half kick him away. Moving Harry firmly to one side, he picked up the man and shook him roughly, then unceremoniously hauled him out into the fresh air, leaving Lucy to struggle to her feet, aided by Harry. Then they heard Sadie's unmistakable giggle as she came in through the side-door.

Lucy stared at her dazedly, hardly hearing Harry asking if she was all right. The drunk she put from her mind—what mattered was that Joe had been in the garden with Sadie!

'Lucy! *Say* something!' Harry was demanding, and Lucy patted her arm gently.

'It's all right, Harry. I'm fine, but thanks for rescuing me. He could have turned tasty.' She gazed unseeingly at Joe as he returned alone. She noticed Sadie put out a hand and clutch at his arm possessively, then, murmuring a hurried 'Excuse me,' Lucy fled to the cloak-room, locking the door firmly behind her, the tears almost choking her. It was certainly a party she would remember for a long time to come!

It was well after midnight when David drove her home. They were both silent, Lucy busy with thoughts of Joe and Sadie kissing in the garden, David probably wondering why she had lost interest in the party and had snapped at him when, a little later, he had tried to introduce her to the very same man who had accosted her in the kitchen!

They had both said things that were better left unsaid, and Lucy felt that this was the beginning of the end. Surprisingly, she felt nothing but relief. If David really did have someone else, then she was happy for him.

'Here we are, back at your own cottage door!' David said lightly a few moments later. 'Not still sulking, are you?'

'Sulking!' Lucy was astonished. She had been about to apologise for snapping at him, even though she'd had plenty of provocation, but to find he had misinterpreted it as sulking was really too much! 'I didn't know I was sulking—surely I have a right to be annoyed by your so-called friend's drunken attentions?' Her voice was icy, and David hastened to placate her.

'I'm sorry. Of course you aren't sulking, but I've already apologised for Ron's behaviour. Anyway, he *was* drunk, and once he's sober he'll be ever so sorry,' he assured her.

'Oh, good, I'm glad about that.' Lucy's biting sarcasm silenced David, for he merely reached across her to open the car door, then sat back, arms folded, while she got out. Then he slammed the door after her, or tried to, but part of her skirt got caught in it and she had to open the door again.

'Sorry,' David muttered, and Lucy, feeling ashamed of her behaviour, put out a hand and gently touched his cheek.

'It's all right, David. I'm sorry, too. This skirt belongs to Sadie, that's the only thing. Oh! What about her? Is Dr Harry bringing her back? I never thought——' No, she hadn't given Sadie another thought. After she had emerged from the cloakroom, the girl had been nowhere in sight, and Lucy had glimpsed her only briefly in the distance after that, talking to Joe and Harry. 'I suppose Harry will bring her back, but I ought to have asked,' she muttered.

'Never mind, love. You had plenty on your mind. Here—how about a goodnight kiss?' David suggested, and Lucy leaned into the car, giving him a more passionate kiss than she would otherwise have done. They were still locked in their uncomfortable embrace when a car tooted loudly behind them, and they were caught full in the glare of its headlights.

The lights were dimmed, and a flushed and embarrassed Lucy broke away. At least it was only Harry and Sadie! How awful if Joe had seen her! 'Goodnight, David. I'll see you!' She backed out of the car, then watched in horror as Harry and Sadie got out of the car behind, followed by the driver—it was Joe!

'Hello there!' Harry waved, a big grin on her face, as well as she might have. 'Did you enjoy the party?'

'Yes, thank you. I had a wonderful time,' Lucy replied woodenly. 'Are you coming in for coffee?'

'That was the general idea,' Joe put in. He sounded amused, and Lucy's temper rose.

'You'd better come in, then. I expect Dad will still be up.' No sooner were the words out of her mouth than the front door opened, and they were being welcomed inside. But it wasn't her dearly loved father who stood there; it was her mother, and Lucy was rooted to the spot.

'Well, well,' Joe murmured, just loud enough for her ears alone. 'Company all round tonight.' He put a hand on Lucy's shoulder and gently propelled her forward, his fingers burning her through the thin blouse, but never had his touch been so welcome.

If it hadn't been for Joe, Lucy didn't know how she would have coped. Naturally she was delighted to see her mother again, but. . .but it would have been better if someone had told me she was coming, Lucy thought as she kissed the cheek her mother offered, and was enfolded in a heavily perfumed embrace.

'You look a real swell in that outfit! Doesn't she, Sadie, love?' Her mother turned her attention to Sadie, without waiting for an answer, then swung round as if she'd had an afterthought, and peered at the gold chains Lucy was wearing.

'Aren't they Sadie's? I felt sure you had some like that, Sadie,' her mother murmured, and both girls tensed.

'They *are* my chains, Mam,' Sadie said blithely, 'and that's my skirt—but I'm wearing Lucy's brooch, so we're even!'

'Oh, good.' Her mother sounded bewildered.

Then her father put in, 'That isn't Lucy's brooch! It's Sadie's! Lucy never wears it and I gave it to——'

'That's Lucy's brooch! My mother left it to her!' the woman put in, icily, and Lucy wanted to cover her ears. It was back to the beginning, all right!

'Sadie and I will share the brooch, Mum. Now, if you'd all sit down, we'll see to the coffee. Do you want to help, Harry?'

With a hearty sigh, Harry joined them in the kitchen, and they fell about with helpless laughter. 'It's quite like old times,' Lucy commented once she was in control again. 'If Dad thinks having Mum back will be heaven, he's got another think coming! Never mind, I expect they enjoy their arguments, really.' It was probably true, she thought ruefully as she went in search of biscuits. It was only she herself who hadn't enjoyed them, the unfortunate child in the middle.

When they returned to the sitting-room with a trolley laden with coffee, biscuits and a cake Sadie had made that morning, they found Joe and Lucy's mother getting on well. Indeed, they were so deep in their reminiscences that her father had retreated into a corner, obviously feeling left out, and he greeted their return with a loud cheer, causing Joe to glance up. His eyes met Lucy's and there was tenderness as well as amusement in his glance.

Surprisingly, she was able to enjoy the rest of the evening, putting everything that had upset her to the back of her mind. If Joe chose to go strolling in the garden with Sadie, what business was it of hers? She ought to warn the girl, tell her not to let the moonlight go to her head, not to be swayed by Joe's dangerous charm; but she was of age, she must make her own decisions, go her own way even if that way was a cul-de-sac as far as a future with Joe Kingsley went.

Even her parents had stopped bickering by the time the party broke up, and a weary Lucy saw Joe and Harry out. Joe paused on the threshold, while Harry went on ahead. 'Be happy, little Lucy,' he whispered huskily, then brushed his lips against her cheek before hurrying after his colleague.

Wonderingly, Lucy put her hand up to her cheek, and stood like that as Joe's car moved out into the night. Then they were gone, but still she lingered. Be happy, little Lucy. Yes, she could be, but only with Joe.

CHAPTER EIGHT

SIDE by side, Lucy and Joe strolled to his car. They were at last able to have their tour of the Shakespeare 'hotspots' as Joe laughingly termed them, and he couldn't have picked a better day. Lucy glanced up appreciatively at the blue, blue sky with its attendant wisps of white clouds. The sun shone gently down upon them, and the only jarring note, in Lucy's estimation, was that they weren't to be alone; this precious, perfect day must be shared with Dr Harry.

Yet, wasn't that as it should be? Love, real love, wasn't selfish. It grew, expanded to embrace everyone, and she couldn't begrudge Harry her treat.

The car was empty, and Lucy turned to Joe in surprise. 'No Harry? When I saw her yesterday she was looking forward to the trip,' she persisted, ashamed of the fact that she was glad to have Joe to herself.

Her happiness was short-lived. 'She's still coming, don't worry, Lucy. She's been delayed, that's all. You knew about the party of American doctors coming to see the unit, didn't you?'

'Mm, yes, Harry told me. She seemed in a fluster about it, but I suppose she might know some of them.' Lucy supplied the answer to her own question, and to her surprise Joe didn't comment.

'I've brought a picnic hamper for teatime—I hope that meets with your approval?' Joe raised a brow, and

Lucy tensed, memories of picnics in that summer long ago coming back to haunt her.

'Yes, lovely,' she agreed, then heard his soft laughter. He was hateful! He must remember one picnic in particular, though she wondered if men *did* remember. Joe must have picnicked with a good many girls since then—why should he recall one in particular?

But he did. 'We used to go picnicking, didn't we?' he commented, as he settled her into the front seat of the car. 'Do you remember?'

It was tempting to say she didn't, that she'd had so many picnics since then that she couldn't be expected to remember, but she couldn't say that to him. 'Yes, I remember,' she said softly. 'I remember a lot of good times we had, Joe, but that's all in the past.'

'Is it? I'm glad,' he said, and, perversely, she was annoyed.

'I thought we'd see the sights in Stratford first, then do Anne Hathaway's cottage later, if there's time. Is that OK with you?' Joe turned to her, his face only inches from her own, and her eyes widened. It would be so easy to reach out and touch him.

'Fine. Where do we start?'

Joe considered for a moment, wanting everything to be right for Lucy. 'We could begin with Shakespeare's birthplace, or would you prefer to see Hall's Croft? New Place?'

'A stroll by the river would be nice,' Lucy suggested hopefully, and Joe chuckled, patting her hand in what she considered an avuncular fashion, before starting the car.

They strolled companionably by the river, to Holy Trinity Church. The sun continued to shine and Lucy felt relaxed, happy, her arm linked through Joe's. It was easy to forget for a moment that she had no claim to him, that Harry would be joining them for lunch, and that in the background was Rosemary, plus the ever-persistent Sadie. Indeed, the instant Sadie heard about the trip she had wanted to come, and had looked so crestfallen when Lucy had told her the day out was solely for Harry's benefit that she had nearly relented. After all, there was room enough for her in the car, and Joe wouldn't have minded—hadn't he suggested inviting her?

They left the crowded church and stood, drinking in the perfect riverside scene. The beauty of nature was almost too much for Lucy, and she turned involuntarily towards Joe, wanting to share her pleasure in the day. He moved towards her at the very same moment, and they stood, lost in their own little world.

Tentatively, Lucy put out her hand and reached up to smooth his cheek. 'Thank you for bringing me today, Joe. It's—it's perfect.' Her voice wasn't quite steady, and Joe let out a sigh that was almost a groan, before bending his head and merely touching her lips with his own.

'No, thank *you*, little Lucy. Or may I call you my little flower?' he asked, the laughter back in his voice, and she joined in.

'You may, just for today,' she agreed. After a long moment they resumed their stroll, taking their time and forgetting all about old houses, and were late meeting Harry at the restaurant Joe had chosen.

The doctor eyed them sharply but made no comment. Indeed, Harry seemed preoccupied still, and Lucy wondered whether she was annoyed at Joe's obvious interest in herself. No, that couldn't be it; Harry hadn't been herself for a few days.

Lucy was determined to chase away Harry's fit of the blues and succeeded to some extent. After an excellent luncheon in a little restaurant overlooking the Avon, they began their tour, Harry insisting on being taken to Holy Trinity Church first, then on to view Shakespeare's birthplace, where they spent so long that Joe had to urge them away.

Harry was lost in wonder at the smallness of the rooms and furniture. 'It must have been kinda cramped for people like me,' she said, tongue-in-cheek, and Lucy giggled.

'I think they were all about *my* height in those days! Even I feel closed in, though,' Lucy acknowledged as they made their way out to rejoin Joe. She wasn't over-fond of tramping around old houses, or any houses come to that; it was other people's gardens that fascinated her, and that was one point in the Shakespeare properties' favour—the old-fashioned, colourful gardens were always a special feature.

They hadn't left enough time to see everything, so settled for seeing Hall's Croft, where Shakespeare's daughter had reputedly lived with her husband, and Harvard House, which Harry was naturally keen to visit.

Laden with souvenirs for Harry to send back home, they were on their way to Harvard House, when Joe hurriedly left them, pleading an important phone call.

Harry gazed after him fondly. 'I thought about reminding him he had to call Rosemary, but he seemed to be enjoying himself so much, I decided against it,' she admitted candidly.

'It isn't like him to forget a thing like that,' Lucy murmured, her mind going numb. Rosemary again. And today had been so perfect! Suddenly the sun went behind a cloud, though a glance up at the sky assured her that it was still up there, shining away. It felt as if it had gone behind a cloud, anyway—a big black rain cloud at that!

'Lucy?' Harry's voice came from far away, and Lucy roused herself.

'Sorry, I was miles away.' Her voice sounded forlorn, even to her own ears, and she quickly pulled herself together.

Joe returned soon after, a happy smile on his face, and Lucy carefully guarded her expression, not wanting him to know how hurt she was. She rather wondered why he hadn't invited Rosemary instead of herself, but she found out the answer a few minutes later.

'She's OK, then? No complications after the op?' Harry asked him, in a low voice.

'No, she's fine, thank you, Harry,' Joe affirmed. Lucy wondered whether Rosemary's operation had been a major one, but didn't like to ask, and Joe said no more on the subject. Instead, they had their picnic tea, then finished the day by driving out to Warwick, Joe promising Harry a trip to Warwick Castle when work next permitted.

'After all, you can't go back home and tell your folks you didn't see a real English castle, can you?' Joe teased her good-humouredly, but mention of home caused Harry's face to fall.

'No, that's right,' she agreed readily enough, but a puzzled Lucy put in,

'You aren't going back yet, surely? You've only just arrived!'

'Well——' Harry hesitated, then shrugged. 'I expected to stay for a year, but circumstances have changed. I guess I'll have to play it by ear,' she said, leaving Lucy more puzzled then before.

Joe dropped Harry off first. She had a flat at the Weston, and refused Lucy's offer of coffee at home. 'That's real sweet of you, Lucy, but I have some letters to write. I don't know where my off duty goes to,' she said ruefully, then blew a kiss to Joe before hurrying into the Weston, leaving an uneasy Lucy wondering whether to invite Joe back home. She didn't want to encourage Sadie, but on the other hand she didn't really want the day to end. It was going to be the last time she accepted an invitation to spend her off duty with Joe, she was adamant about that, and she wanted to prolong this day if she possibly could.

'Shall we go back to your father's?' Joe asked easily. 'Or will you come out to see the cottage? It's only rented and I'd like your opinion. It's coming on the market shortly and I was thinking of making the owner an offer.'

Lucy was perfectly sure that it wasn't a good idea to see Joe's home, to be alone with him there, but she was going to take the risk. When he had worked at the hospital before, he had lived in the doctors' residence, but now, he told her, he had the cottage to call home. 'Temporarily, anyway. When the scheme gets under way I might go back up north. I haven't decided yet,' he said, then hesitated as if about to say more, but didn't, and Lucy was left wondering whether Rosemary's plans might influence his own.

A few miles further on, they began to follow a narrow, twisting road that ended rather abruptly in a lane which was little better than a cart-track. 'This lane won't be too great in the winter,' he said laconically, and Lucy smiled, despite herself.

'That's the understatement of the year, I should think! Oh—Joe, it's beautiful!' Just as the lane seemed about to peter out, the cottage came into view. It stood aloof in the middle of a wild garden, with a straggly orchard running along one side. The cottage seemed to grow out of the garden, like something out of Lewis Carroll, its two diamond-paned windows like surprised eyes, its cheerful red door a welcoming mouth.

Perhaps the cottage was enchanted, and certainly Lucy was. 'I never imagined. . .' She was lost for words. If ever there was a case of love at first sight, this was it! She wouldn't have been at all surprised to see the white rabbit come prancing out of the door, or the Cheshire cat sit grinning a welcome from the front step.

Joe chuckled, enjoying her surprise. 'Now you know why I'm thinking of offering for it. It's pricey, though,' he went on, and Lucy could well believe that. He let her out, then swung the car round, heading for a huge barn which evidently did duty as a garage.

Lucy glanced down at the house keys he had thrust into her hands. If these were Joe's keys then they were also Rosemary's. Whether they lived together now or not, there would be something of Rosemary in the cottage. She hesitated for a moment, feeling herself to be an interloper, and waited until Joe came striding towards her before quickly slipping the key into the lock on the stout front door.

Joe followed her in, closing the door decisively behind him. It seemed to Lucy that he was closing everyone out and that they were the only two people left in the entire world.

Such thoughts had their dangers, and she quickly made her way along a long, narrow hall towards what she hoped was the kitchen. And what a kitchen! 'Oh, Joe! Sadie's mouth would water if she could see this! She's always moaning because Dad's kitchen's much smaller than Mum's,' she went on, hardly knowing what she was saying, as she set out to explore the big, square room. Tucked away against the further wall was a small breakfast bar, with gaily coloured stools and coffee-making equipment at the ready, and double-glazed doors opening on to a paved patio. They commanded a view of a garden which seemed to stretch endlessly into the distance—an appealingly overgrown garden.

'I need a gardener. Your Sadie isn't a dab hand at gardening, too, is she? She seems to score ten out of ten at everything else,' Joe said drily, and Lucy bit her lip, trying not to laugh.

'I do go on a bit about her accomplishments, don't I? I promise not to mention her again!'

'It's just that she adores, baking, sewing and house-work and positively *loves* showing old ladies across the road, and is absolutely *marvellous* at everything else under the sun! Yes, I know, and quite frankly she bores me!' Joe said firmly. 'Anyway, you weren't fishing for compliments for yourself, were you? I dare say you have one or two accomplishments Sadie hasn't got,' he added silkily, and Lucy flushed.

'That's not fair, Joe! Anyway, we won't quarrel. Can I see over the garden?' she asked, anxious to get out of the cottage. Feeling that it was her own weakness for Joe that was the danger factor, she hurried out through the double doors and went lightly down the steps, then stopped, just drinking in the beauty. True, it *did* need a gardener's firm hand but she thought it lovely just as it was. It was the garden of her dreams, for, just as she thought it had given up all its secrets, she found the sundial. Forlorn and forgotten, it stood in the middle of a little stone-paved rockery, and Lucy perched on a rock and closed her eyes, lifting her face to the evening sun. This was the perfect ending to a perfect day. Or would be, if the dark shadow that was Rosemary Kingsley wasn't drifting around the garden.

It's Rosemary's home, not yours, Lucy could hear an inner voice saying, but she chose to ignore it, just for a few moments longer. This day with Joe was little enough—surely Rosemary wouldn't begrudge her that?

She was sitting by the sundail, idly swinging her foot and letting her mind relax, when Joe found her. She didn't see him at first, and he was able to watch her, his expression grave. He'd been a damn fool to bring her here, yet he had wanted to see her in the setting of his own home, or what he was beginning to think of as his own. The wild beauty of the north-country called him from time to time, but home was where the heart was, and his heart was right here—with Lucy. Yet what could he offer her? Once before, his need for her had spilled over into what he now thought of as a

tawdry affair. She was so young, so trusting! She
obviously cared for him, but how much? Not enough
to take on a lonely, embittered man, a workaholic, a
man with one failed marriage behind him, a man who
couldn't. . .

No. He shook his head, then, shrugging, walked
slowly down to where Lucy still sat, oblivious of the
emotion raging within him. No, Lucy was young for
her years, and there was that Asher chap. She would
be better off with him. And there was still
Rosemary. . .

'Hello!' Lucy smiled warmly into his eyes. 'You
didn't tell me you had a sundial!'

Joe's face clouded, but he stared obligingly at the
sundial for a moment. 'The hands haven't moved yet,'
he complained, and Lucy chuckled.

'You are a fool, Joe! I'm sure the hands of my watch
haven't moved, either. It's—it's so. . .' She waved a
hand vaguely, trying to encompass the beauty of the
summer evening, the garden, the peace and serenity
everywhere. 'I'm afraid I haven't the words,' she
admitted, feeling foolish, but Joe seemed to
understand.

'I think "timeless" is the word you're looking for—
now you know why I want to buy the place.' Deliberately he turned the conversation to mundane matters,
and Lucy was content to give him her opinion about
the decorations, how much of the garden ought to be
tamed, whether or not he should build a proper garage,
and so on. It was safer that way, she knew, far safer,
even though her unruly tongue longed to tell him how
much she was enjoying his company. The sun had lost
its warmth, though, and with rain forecast for the

following day Lucy knew her heaven was drawing to its close.

Abruptly she rose, lacing her fingers together nervously, not wanting him to think she was anxious to go. 'I've had a really lovely day, Joe. Thank you—for everything,' she said simply, then wondered at the expression of pain that crossed his face. Probably he was glad to get rid of her. There was Rosemary to be considered after all. He must be wanting to get to the hospital to see his wife.

His wife. Or, more likely, his ex-wife, Lucy conceded. She doubted that he would have brought her to the home he shared with another woman. 'I'd better get back,' she rushed on, and Joe nodded morosely. He had been about to kiss her, but was glad now he hadn't given in to the temptation. It could have led anywhere, but he knew where he wanted it to lead.

'Yes, I'll get the car out. Oh—would you like a coffee? I meant to show you over my dream home but we seem to have got side-tracked,' he admitted.

'Never mind, I'm not that much interested in seeing over other people's homes, strange though it may seem,' Lucy told him. 'It's gardens that attract me. Now gardening *is* something I'm quite good at!'

'Good! I needn't worry that the redoubtable Sadie will turn up on my doorstep tomorrow morning armed with garden tools and a wheelbarrow!' Joe said feelingly, and Lucy couldn't keep her laughter back.

But her laughter died when she accurately read the expression on Joe's face, and she hastily backed away. There was no mistaking the pain in his eyes this time.

'Don't worry, Staff Nurse Powell—I'm not going to overpower you and carry you off protesting to my chamber!' Joe's laughter had faded and he was once more Professor Joe Kingsley. And it was all her fault.

'I can get a taxi home, if you'd rather.' Lucy's voice was cold, distant now, her expression daunting to even the bravest heart, and Joe silently cursed.

'No, I'll drive you back. I have to go into town, anyway.'

'Yes, of course. Rosemary,' Lucy murmured, forgetting for a moment that she hadn't intended mentioning her.

He looked surprised. 'Yes, Rosemary. She's had a hysterectomy at the Central. I promised to spend the rest of the evening there.' Deliberately, he glanced at his watch. 'There won't be much evening left by the time I arrive. I'll get a rocket,' he said, a little smile in his voice, and Lucy nodded, numbly.

They were silent on the drive home, Lucy not wanting to say anything that would cause even more bad feeling between them, and Joe knowing he mustn't tell her how he felt.

He hesitated as he dropped her outside her house. It was twilight now, a time meant for lovers. Something in her expression must have told him how full her heart was, for he leaned towards her and kissed her on the mouth.

'Have fun, little Lucy,' he whispered.

'Of course! I always do,' she answered brightly.

She got out of the car, not glancing back but knowing that Joe was waiting until she was safely indoors. It gave her the feeling of being cared for—if only he *did* care for her!

CHAPTER NINE

'ARE all the doctors here, Edna?' Lucy asked a few days later, as they snatched a couple of minutes' break. The unit was fairly humming with activity and Lucy was glad of it: anything was better than having time on her hands and nothing much to occupy her mind—except the devastating knowledge that she was beginning to love Joe more and more with each passing day. Something would have to be done—but what? She just didn't know. Short of resigning from a job she enjoyed and felt was a challenge, there was no way she could avoid almost daily contact with Joe Kingsley.

Edna Shepham nodded. 'There seems like hundreds, but it should be only twenty. Most are Americans, but there's one from Japan, and another two from Sweden. Where's our Joe? Have you seen him lately?'

'He was here a few minutes ago—the last time I saw him he was heading for X-ray,' Lucy said. Apart from at work, she hadn't seen anything of Joe, but she knew someone who had—Sadie. And that surprised as well as annoyed her. After Joe's remarks about Sadie getting on his nerves, Lucy had been shocked to learn that Joe was taking her to the theatre. That was last night and when Lucy asked her if she had enjoyed the evening Sadie had just giggled.

That giggle was gnawing away at her insides now. If Joe thought so little of Sadie, why had he taken her out? And what about Rosemary? It seemed to her that

141

he enjoyed taking everyone out, except herself! Then both women glanced up as Joe hovered in the doorway of the little staff-room, a petulant-looking David Asher just behind him.

'Ready for the reception, ladies?'

'Yes, all ready,' Edna agreed. 'Oh—what about Harry? Shouldn't she be here?'

'Yes, she should be but I let her off, just this once.' Joe's voice was distant, and both women knew better than to question his decision. Perhaps Harry wasn't feeling too well, though Lucy felt there was more to it than that. Harry had been positively agitated recently, and Lucy was worried, wondering if there was bad news from home.

'You're looking fierce, Staff Nurse,' Joe commented, then picked up the notes that Edna handed him and walked off with her, leaving Lucy momentarily alone with David.

'Hello, stranger!' Lucy smiled at him, trying to coax a smile in return, and David shrugged, then dropped a light kiss on her brow, after first glancing back into the corridor to make sure they weren't observed.

'Yes, I am a stranger! You'd be surprised at the amount of work the old man generates! The man's a workaholic,' he said bitterly.

'I thought you knew that? Anyway, you won't be here much longer, will you? Have you told him?'

David looked uncomfortable. 'No, not yet. I haven't got to make a final decision until I come back from the course, but I expect he knows I'm less than enchanted.'

'But why? He doesn't ask you to do more than he does himself!' Lucy cried. 'And as for rearranging the schedules, I thought that left you with more free time, not less!'

David looked startled, as well he might, Lucy thought crossly. He was always complaining that he never got any free time now, but Lucy knew very well he had. And knew where and with whom he was spending that time. Heather had seen David and the relief sister from Shakespeare ward together several times and hadn't failed to mention it to her. That had solved the puzzle, anyway. She had been wondering about Ron's remarks at the party and now she knew— the sister was a pretty platinum blonde!

'I suppose it isn't that bad,' David admitted, with a quick glance at Lucy's face as if to reassure himself that she didn't know he was two-timing her. 'Anyway, are you coming to the reception? He's that keen on home-care now that I'm surprised he finds time to do anything else,' he added peevishly, and Lucy longed to shake him. The depths of her feelings surprised and alarmed her. If David wanted to behave like a spoiled child, then let him. Joe could manage very well with him.

The reception was for the group of visiting doctors. They were over to watch Joe operate and to attend lectures on surgery, and would be staying for three days, according to Edna. Harry hadn't mentioned them at all, beyond telling Lucy that they had arrived, and she wondered about that. It could be that one of them was Harry's ex-husband, since Lucy knew he was a surgeon. Well, it wasn't any of her business. She couldn't even settle her own future, and certainly wasn't about to meddle in Harry's!

The common-room was buzzing with conversation by the time she got there. There was no sign of Joe, but Edna Shepham waved to her and Lucy made her way towards her.

'Joe's disappeared, yet I would have sworn he was headed straight this way,' Edna commented, glancing at her watch. 'We're already behind and that's not like him. I stopped off on paeds to have a word with the sister there and I thought he would have been here. Still, not to worry,' Edna went on, but when Lucy volunteered to look for Joe her offer was eagerly accepted.

Lucy decided to look in his office. Perhaps a query had arisen about a patient. As she paused uncertainly outside his office door she heard his voice, and was about to knock, but didn't need to. The door was sufficiently ajar for her to see for herself—Joe and Dr Harry were standing in the middle of the room, and Joe had her face cradled in his hands as he gazed down at her.

'Oh, Harry! What am I going to do about you?' he murmured, then bent his head, at which point Lucy crept away, shaken to the core.

Joe and Harry! Of course; at first she had thought they might have had a romance while they were in the States, but knew that she'd been mistaken—they were simply friends. As Joe had said, no one could help liking Harry—but now. . .

Now Harry had fallen in love with Joe, and he with her. The realisation hit Lucy like a douche of cold water, and she was incapable of answering Edna when she asked if Joe was on his way. Then she roused herself, seeing Edna's look of alarm. 'Yes, he's just coming. I think he was detained,' she murmured, and Edna seemed satisfied.

Indeed, he arrived less than five minutes later, but they were the longest five minutes of Lucy's life. Harry wasn't with him, but she wasn't surprised. It wouldn't do for a doctor to arrive looking as though she had just been kissed—and Harry had surely just been kissed.

To Lucy's surprise, Dr Harry did turn up shortly afterwards, looking subdued but otherwise her usual self. Despite being fully occupied, she kept an eye on Harry and wasn't surprised when a tall, well-built doctor headed that way, though, even from where she stood, Lucy could see that Harry wasn't too pleased.

A few minutes later, Lucy herself came face to face with the tall American who had held such a terse conversation with Harry.

'You know Dr Hamilton, then?' Lucy began, and the doctor nodded grimly.

'Yes, you could say that,' he admitted.

'You wouldn't be her ex-husband, by any chance?' Lucy asked boldly.

'Well, yes I *would* be,' he said, with a slow grin. 'At least, I *am*, but I'd rather not be,' he amended.

'It isn't any of my business, but I hope you won't upset Harry; she hasn't been herself lately,' Lucy rushed on.

'That's too bad,' he murmured. 'My name's Ray Simmons, and you must be little Lucy,' he went on, astonishing her.

Of course, her name was clearly printed on her name badge, but how did he know about 'little Lucy'? 'Yes, I suppose I am,' she agreed, and he smiled, his slow careful smile, which Lucy found very engaging. Whatever the problems in the past, she hoped he and Harry might get back together again. Then she recalled that scene in Joe's office, and her face fell. But perhaps Harry had turned to Joe on the rebound? Yes, that must be it! Once she had a chance to talk to Ray again, sort out their differences, Harry might find she really *did* still love him.

With that end in view, Lucy asked him to take round a plate of sausage rolls for her, and gently pushed him in Harry's direction. He needed no prodding, and Lucy mentally crossed her fingers as he approached his ex-wife. Then one of the female doctors claimed her attention, and she saw no more of the couple.

At length Joe detached himself from the group of doctors and approached her, grim-faced. Lucy paused in the act of emptying out some packets of crisps, her face lighting up at sight of him. 'I'm that rushed off my feet I haven't had time to eat yet. Are you hungry, Professor?'

'Hungry?' Joe raked his fingers through his hair, making it look untidier than ever. 'No, not particularly,' he went on, his expression harassed. 'Have you seen Harry?' he demanded, and Lucy started to shake her head, then remembered Ray.

'She was here a while back,' she answered evasively, waving her hand in the direction of the others. 'Are you sure you don't want anything? I saved you a few sandwiches.'

'No, I do *not* want any food. Thank you, Staff Nurse,' Joe said coldly, his eyes already searching the throng for Harry and not finding her.

Lucy went cold. Joe obviously couldn't wait to see Harry again, but then, what did she expect? 'She was near her ex-husband when I saw her last,' she admitted, and Joe swung round, his heavy brows drawn together in a frown.

'Ray? Was she? That surprises me, little Lucy.' His tone was amused rather than angry, but before Lucy could comment he left her, and made his way slowly through the gathering. She still couldn't see Harry, or Ray Simmons. It seemed they had stepped outside to talk things over. From Joe's urgency to see Harry again, this must be the very thing he was afraid of, and Lucy's heart went out to him. She knew only too well how it felt to be the one who loved but who was not loved in return.

The guests were beginning to disperse by the time she caught sight of Harry again. She was deep in conversation with Joe, and of her ex-husband there was no sign. When Joe nodded in Lucy's direction, Harry made her way purposefully towards her.

'Joe found you, then,' she said swiftly as Harry approached.

'Yes, he rescued me from my ex,' Harry said bluntly. 'The more I see that guy, the happier I am that we divorced,' she added meaningfully, and Lucy coloured.

'Sorry, it was my fault, I suppose. I sent him on his way with a few snacks—but he seemed so nice!' Lucy went on crossly, tired of apologising. If Harry couldn't hold her marriage together, it really wasn't fair to blame anyone else.

'He is nice. I like him,' Harry admitted with a little smile that gave Lucy reason to hope. 'But there's nothing deader than yesterday's flame, Lucy. Remember that.'

'Yes, I know,' Lucy said with a bright smile. 'You can't breathe life back into a fire that's been dead for—

for years.' She turned to survey the clutter left by the visitors. 'Do you think we ought to help clear up? I know the domestics will do it, but it seems unfair to leave it all to them.'

'Yes, it does,' Harry agreed. 'We'll gather everything together, shall we? It will give me something to do.'

To Lucy's surprise, Joe joined them in tidying up, while Harry, despite saying she wanted to help, did nothing but wander around vaguely for a while, then absently pick up an empty glass and stare into it. Evidently, seeing her ex-husband had upset her more than she was prepared to admit.

Joe's quizzical gaze was also on Harry, but he stayed with Lucy, and they worked side by side in a companionable silence that made her heart feel lighter than it had done for days. The scene in Joe's office she pushed to the back of her mind.

'The domestic supervisor will probably call her ladies out on strike,' Joe commented lightly as they stood back to survey their handiwork.

'Probably,' Lucy agreed, laughter in her voice. 'I'd better get on, I suppose. I promised I would call on Peter Elliott before I go off duty,' she put in, unnerved by his silent scrutiny, and he frowned.

'Why, for heaven's sake? He's got his home-care nurses! You can't be everywhere,' he pointed out, then put his hand under her elbow and guided her out of the room, leaving Harry still staring into space.

'Joe—Professor,' Lucy began, 'I promised, and if you promise a patient something you should never let them down!'

'Don't lecture me, Staff Nurse!' Joe knew he was

being unreasonably angry, but Lucy was taking too much extra work upon herself.

'I apologise, sir,' she said stiffly, her eyes sparking, and Joe grinned.

'You don't look apologetic, Staff Nurse Powell,' he said easily.

'Well, no, I find it difficult,' Lucy admitted with a smile, her good humour restored. 'Anyway, if you'd rather I didn't visit, then I won't. I mentioned him to Heather—I thought she would be just the person to bring him out of himself,' she added, and Joe nodded gravely.

'By all means go, if you must—no, wait. Let the male nurse go. Nurse Atkins, isn't it? Yes, give him a ring, Lucy. Now I have to sort poor Harry out.' With that, he retaced his steps, leaving Lucy, her mind in a whirl, wondering just what sorting out he had in mind for Harry.

'Lucy! Wait!'

She swung round, her face lighting up, but it was David, not Joe, who came hurrying out after her. 'Hello, I thought you were still with our guests. Do you want a lift somewhere?' She was pleased to see him, nevertheless, and they fell into step as she went to her car.

'I thought we might make a night of it,' David suggested diffidently. 'If you're not too tired, that is,' he went on quickly, and Lucy shot him a puzzled glance.

'What happened to Sister Shakespeare?' she asked tartly, and David reddened, then waved a hand vaguely.

'It was only a friendship, Lucy. There's no need to read too much into it,' he said irritably.

'No, if you say so,' Lucy said equably, not really caring either way. 'Anyway, as it happens, I'd love a night on the town.' She surprised herself as much as David by accepting his invitation. Seeing Harry and Joe together was a bitter pill to swallow—what better than an evening's entertainment to sweeten the pill?

Despite Joe's instructions to phone the male nurse, Lucy decided to visit Peter Elliott herself. She had seen him once since his discharge, since she liked to see for herself that the scheme was operating smoothly. The home circumstances hadn't improved, with Peter and his brother-in-law still at loggerheads, but the social worker was very supportive, and Peter's sister knew she could ring Lucy or Edna Shepham at any time for a chat or advice.

For a change, though, Peter looked remarkably cheerful when he came to the door. 'Well, if it isn't my guardian angel! Come in, love. I've got a friend with me,' he said in a much lower tone, and Lucy's eyes glinted with laughter.

'A female friend, would that be?' she whispered back.

'Come and meet her,' Peter suggested, leading the way into the kitchen, where, to Lucy's surprise, she found Peter's sister and a tall young woman she had no difficulty in recognising—Carol Barrett!

Carol was delighted to see her, but made sure that Lucy understood she was only visiting. Peter's sister looked even more harassed than usual, but she and Carol seemed to be getting on reasonably well.

'I'm glad you've found a friend, Peter,' Lucy said

warmly. Carol might not have been everyone's idea of a friend, but if she was willing to accept Peter as he was it would do them both the world of good.

After a quick coffee, Lucy made her escape before the pair could unload any more problems on to her. This was the first time she'd seen Carol since her discharge from hospital. Accommodation had been found for her in the town, and patient—and problems—had passed out of their hands.

Lucy had wanted to call on Mrs Welford, but Peter had taken up too much time. There were never enough hours in the day, and she began to wish she had turned down David's invitation.

'*Marry* you?' Lucy stared blankly at David, who looked annoyed.

'Yes, marry me, get hitched, tie the knot—become my wife,' he went on stolidly. 'You look as if I've suggested running a house of ill repute!'

'I was startled, that's all, though perhaps "astounded" would be a better word,' she went on sharply. 'You carry on with another nurse, you pretend you're working when you aren't, and now, out of the blue, you propose to *me*! What am I supposed to think?'

Once she might have been glad to marry David. Despite their differences, they got on well enough, and if she couldn't have Joe then David was surely an acceptable substitute. . . No, she acknowledged, no one was a substitute for Joe Kingsley, and she found herself refusing, gently but firmly.

'I can't imagine why you want to marry me after all this time,' she carried on, 'especially as you——'

'I *have* proposed before, you may recall,' he said stiffly. 'Twice, as far as I can remember.'

'That's true, but you know you didn't mean it. You can't afford to marry yet, you've always said so,' Lucy pointed out, then impulsively put out her hand and patted his clenched fist, her fingers gently easing his apart. 'Don't get uptight about it—you didn't really think that was the answer, did you? If your other girlfriend has let you down, marriage to me would only be love on the rebound. And that wouldn't work,' she said hollowly, her eyes far away. No, that certainly wouldn't work. '*Has* she let you down? she asked, curiosity getting the better of her, then watched as David turned brick-red and snatched his hand away.

'No! It's nothing like that. It's just that—that——' He stopped, and Lucy waited. 'If I want to get on in my career, old Ivor said I ought to get married. Nothing like a good steady wife to stabilise an up-and-coming doctor, he said,' David mumbled, and Lucy began to see.

'Ah! It's Mr Browne I have to thank for the proposal, is it? It still won't work, David. You can't marry a woman you don't love, and I——'

'But I do love you!' he blurted out, clutching her hand again. 'Haven't I said so?'

'No, not as far as I can remember,' Lucy said truthfully.

'That's it, start getting clever! Oh, Lucy, I didn't mean that, but until old Geordie Joe showed up again we had something going for us, didn't we?'

Misery stared out of David's eyes, and Lucy looked away, knowing the truth of what he said. Until Joe had come back she and David were almost in love, certainly good friends. Might that not have turned to love? Marriages, successful ones, had been built on less. True, it wasn't very romantic, but romance didn't pay the bills. But, after Joe, could she ever fall in love again? Could she marry another man? That heady romance had spoiled her for anyone else. In Joe's arms she had found paradise, albeit a temporary one. She had been swept along on a raging tide of emotion, had reached new heights of passion, and plumbed the depths of misery, certainly, but at least there had been nothing tame about their relationship! With Joe, being just good friends simply would not have been enough.

'I——' She stopped, suddenly becoming aware of the man himself. How she had sensed his presence in the restaurant she didn't know, but she had casually glanced across the room and there he was—just taking his place a few tables away, with Harry Hamilton! 'It wouldn't work,' she repeated slowly, her mind in a daze.

Now it was David's turn to comfort her. Gently he squeezed her hand, leaning towards her. 'It *would* work, Lucy. You know I love you—that business. . .that. . .it's over. That's all I can say,' he assured her, and Lucy nodded her acceptance of the fact.

'If you say so, though I'm sorry for you.' And sorry for me, as well, she thought, wondering whether she should acknowledge Joe's presence. She decided she *would* glance up casually and pretend she had only just seen him. When she did so, it was to find that Joe's eyes were already on her, and he half raised his hand in a salute. Harry also turned and beamed across at her. 'That's the old man over by the mirror,' she told

David, proud of the way she kept her voice normal. 'He's with Dr Harry.'

'Aha! Is there a great romance brewing, do you think? I know, we'll invite them to drink to our happiness,' David went on, before Lucy could even open her mouth. To her horror, he went straight across to Joe, and though she couldn't hear what was being said she could see the pleased expression on the consultant's face—Joe was glad she was marrying David! How could he?

Feeling betrayed, Lucy somehow kept a bright smile pinned to her face, not the sort of smile it would have been had Joe proposed to her, but nevertheless a passable imitation of it. David, too, was beaming, as he returned and settled down opposite her. 'The chief's delighted, Lucy. Very pleased, he said. It couldn't happen to two nicer people. That's what he said,' David went on, and Lucy smiled even harder.

Then, when she saw that Joe and Harry had resumed their inspection of the menu, she said quietly, 'It was a pity you hadn't waited to hear *my* opinion of the engagement! I have no intention of marrying you, David! It wouldn't work—you've just agreed with that,' she assured him, and he looked stunned.

'But—but you said you would! Didn't you?'

'No, I did not—you never gave me a chance!' she went on relentlessly. 'We'll just have to play it down and hope they don't spread the glad tidings. You know what the Weston General's grapevine is like,' Lucy went on bitterly. 'That grapevine's caused me a lot of unhappiness in the past; now it looks set to do so in the future! I thought you would have had more sense!' she finished, pushing away her plate and reaching for her

glass of wine. She drank deeply, even though it was
too dry for her taste.

'There's no more to be said, then, is there?' David
said tonelessly. 'I suppose you still fancy our professor?
He seems ready to tie the knot with Harry, you know.
Whatever happened between you in the past,
you——'

'Can't go back. No, I've already been told that a
number of times,' Lucy assured him. 'Perhaps we
should have coffee now? I don't really fancy a
pudding.'

They had finished their meal and were ready to leave
when Joe glanced up, his gaze quizzical, but it was
Harry who came over, her face radiant. 'I couldn't be
happier for you, honey! I really couldn't! You're just
right for each other,' she went on, and Lucy had
difficulty in biting back the retort she wanted to make.

'Yes, but I'm sorry your romance hasn't had a happy
ending—but perhaps it has?' Lucy rushed on, horrified
at herself for asking. She didn't want to know, she
didn't!

Harry shrugged. 'Well. . .time will tell. I may have a
happy ending yet! You just wait and see.'

Since David was in a bad mood, Lucy offered to get
a taxi home, and to her chagrin he didn't protest. They
parted with a barely civil goodbye, and by the time she
arrived home she had the grandmother of all head-
aches. Never mind, at least she hadn't taken second
best. She was still free, and if she couldn't have Joe
Kingsley, then she would remain single. She had her
work, after all.

She arrived at the hospital bright and early the
following morning, intending to drown herself in work,

work and more work. With any luck, news of the
engagement wouldn't leak out, but that idea was
quickly proved wrong because the first person she met
was Heather Baynes, who said she supposed she should
offer her congratulations.

Lucy stared at her for a moment, wondering how
Heather knew. 'On what am I being congratulated?'
she hedged.

'Well, on marrying David! You're certainly a dark
horse, Lucy! I met him in the corridor and——'

'And he told you that?' Lucy blazed, causing her
friend to take a step backward.

'No, *he* didn't, *I* did,' Joe said suavely, strolling into
Lucy's office and smiling wolfishly at her. 'Dr Asher
didn't seem about to mention it, for some reason,' he
continued pleasantly.

'That's because we——' Lucy began, then broke off.
Let him continue to think she was engaged. She hoped
it hurt him as much as his affairs hurt her! 'I hope you
won't go around spreading the glad tidings, Heather?
Or you, Professor?' Lucy said firmly, beginning to sort
some papers on her desk. 'Nothing's settled yet and
David can't really afford to marry right now. Anyway,
there's no point in making a fuss over an engagement,
is there?' Striving to appear happy was more difficult
than it sounded, and Lucy felt she wasn't making a
very good job of it.

'No, all right,' Heather agreed, staring at her in
bewilderment. 'You don't want me to tell all our
friends, then?'

'Oh, no!' Lucy blurted out. 'Not just yet. We want
to keep it to ourselves. It's *our* engagement, after all;
it doesn't belong to anyone else,' she went on foolishly,

and Heather shrugged, then walked away, shaking her head.

'I'd like to wish you every happiness, Lucy,' Joe said softly. 'I'm glad you've found someone your own age,' he added, but before Lucy could speak he went on to talk about the home-care scheme. 'Things aren't going as well as planned, you know,' he began, striding up and down the small room. Lucy's anguished eyes followed him, but each time he turned by the doorway she hastily glanced down at her desk. 'We're getting too many geriatric patients—and that isn't the type of patient the scheme is intended for,' he said, stopping just in front of her.

Lucy nodded without glancing up, and she heard his sharply indrawn breath. 'Look at me when I'm speaking to you, Staff Nurse,' he went on gently, and Lucy looked up, keeping her gaze hooded. 'That's better. I like to see those pretty eyes of yours,' Joe commented, a slight smile on his face. 'Why so sad? I thought girls in love radiated happiness?'

Feeling that he was mocking her did nothing to improve Lucy's temper. 'If you expect me to go around grinning all over my face, then I'm afraid you're in for a disappointment! I told you, we want to keep the engagement private. I'm not sure David's ready to settle down yet, and perhaps I'm not, either,' she went on, picking up her notebook and staring down at it unseeingly. 'What will you do about the elderly patients?'

Accepting the abrupt change of subject, Joe walked away from her and stood leaning against the filing cabinet. 'Call another meeting, for one thing. Then get the GPs organised to send us the type of patient we're supposed to be catering for—the acutely ill, young or middle-aged. Then of course we'll be accused of creaming off the best and easiest patients, leaving the elderly to the care of the overworked district nurses!' He ran his fingers through his hair, leaving it a tousled mop, and Lucy concentrated fiercely on her notebook, her hand poised over a fresh page. 'By the way, they've traced Tom Noble's sister—did Harry tell you? No, she isn't in today,' Joe muttered.

'I heard about it, though. I'm off to check on him this afternoon,' Lucy told him. 'He seems to be coping, anyway. We've got two more old folk going out this week, Professor—you did realise that?'

'Mm? Oh, yes, I know who we've got and why. One of them's in her eighties! Never mind, we'll help her out for a few days. She'll enjoy the extra attention, I expect,' Joe went on wryly, and Lucy's lips parted in a smile.

'I'm going to make her my special pet, even if it *isn't* allowed,' she said, and Joe chuckled, that husky chuckle she loved so much.

'I wish I could be your special pet, little Lucy,' he said softly, his eyes conveying so much more than his words, and Lucy opened her mouth to speak, to tell him he *could*, that she wasn't engaged, she was free, eager and willing, but Sister Shepham appeared just then and the moment was lost—probably forever, Lucy thought glumly as she made her way out to the car park, then realised that it was far too early to be calling on patients in the community. That came of starting work so much earlier than normal people! It wasn't even nine o'clock yet, and she hesitated briefly before making her way back to Arden ward. She could at least talk to some of those who would be discharged this week. It was all Joe's fault. His words had thrown her so much that she didn't know quite *what* she was supposed to be doing, or when!

Tom Noble didn't look the slightest bit pleased to see her that afternoon, but Lucy wasn't daunted—*nothing* seemed to please him!

Her conversation with Joe about a semi-convalescent home for people like Mr Noble and Peter Elliott had borne fruit. The charitable foundation which was paying the home-care nurses had expressed an interest, but they were all under a strict vow of secrecy about it. Money wasn't easily come by and the scheme might die a death. If it didn't, then Tom Noble's future would be assured.

'Has your sister been in touch, Mr Noble?' Lucy asked brightly, as he stood aside reluctantly for her to enter his new bedsitter. It was a big room, bright and airy, but dreadfully untidy, with remains of yesterday's meal still lying on the small table, the bed unmade, the curtains half-drawn to keep out the sunlight.

Lucy's fingers itched to tidy up, but if Mr Noble was happy in his untidy state and there was no health risk it wasn't up to her to interfere.

'Aye, Eleanor's still about,' Mr Noble muttered, staring, perplexed, at the table. 'My landlady's a good soul. She has me down every day for my dinner,' he volunteered.

'If that's yesterday's tea, do you want me to clear it up for you? The birds would be glad of those crusts.' Lucy waited, not making a move, aware that the patient was surveying her covertly from under his sparse brows.

'You're a canny lass,' he muttered. 'Aye, you can clear up. Mrs Mitchell will have a fit if she sees all the mess.' He paused as Lucy got up and took off her suit jacket. 'What did you say your name was? Lucy? Wor Eleanor'll like you, I don't doubt.'

With that, Mr Noble sank into the shabby armchair while a bemused Lucy tidied up. Perhaps *he* was on his way to becoming her special pet!

CHAPTER TEN

LUCY'S mind was busy as she headed back to the unit to write her report. Since yesterday, she and Joe had hardly spoken. His words about wanting to be her special pet had stayed with her for the rest of that day, and she clutched them to her, holding on to them. She must mean something to him, surely?

The man in question was holding an impromptu ward round in Arden as she passed, and Lucy hesitated, knowing she must speak to him as he left the ward because he was off duty for a couple of days after that. Where and with whom he would spend that off duty was a question that had frequently exercised her mind lately, but it wasn't her business. Keep everything strictly professional and her poor heart wouldn't get bumped and bruised again. It shouldn't be too difficult.

'I wanted to see you about Mr Olive, sir, before you go off duty.' Lucy caught up with him as he left the ward, determined to make their meeting as brief as possible.

'Ah, yes, off duty; I can hardly wait,' he commented, and Lucy couldn't tell if he was being sarcastic or actually looking forward to a few days off. Heaven knew, the man deserved it. David was always complaining about the extra hours he'd had to work lately, but Lucy had never once heard Joe complain. He was frequently on the surgical wards long after the rest of the senior staff had left.

Her gaze softened, but unfortunately Joe glanced up at that moment, and she looked away, embarrassed. Edna's eyes were busily scanning case-notes, and there was no one else in the little office to notice, but Joe had, and that was enough.

'Mr Olive—Fred Olive.' Edna Shepham spoke into the lengthening silence, then rose with a rustle of starched apron. 'I had a feeling he was about to change his GP, but I'm not sure. I'd better ask him,' she muttered, walking briskly out, and Lucy hesitated, not wanting to be alone with Joe any longer than she could help. 'Mr Olive—will he be discharged tomorrow? I've lined up a nurse to visit him, but he's such a difficult man and I don't——'

'Difficult patients get more attention, unfortunately,' Joe said drily, 'but he *will* be a problem. If he's changing his doctor again, we must make sure the right one's told we're discharging him. That's where there could be a breakdown in care. And any lack of communication will be blamed on us, naturally.'

Lucy murmured her agreement. 'I'd better see him myself, then.' She made for the door, but Joe's voice stopped her.

'No, wait, Lucy. Since we're quieter now, I may take a little longer, combine my days off with a holiday,' he went on, and Lucy's eyes widened in dismay. 'I thought I might go back up north, see a few old friends,' he said, his gaze intent. 'We must have a celebration dinner before I go, though—how are you fixed for tonight? Or is lover-boy wining and dining you?'

Lucy opened her mouth in astonishment. 'Celebration dinner?'

'To celebrate your engagement. If you have to keep

it quiet, you can't be planning an engagement party, so I thought I'd remedy that by inviting you to dinner. But perhaps the idea doesn't appeal?' he suggested coolly.

'Oh, you mean both of us!' Lucy's face cleared. 'Yes, I expect if David can get away. . .he's been on lates and—oh, you know that.' She halted in confusion, having been about to tell her chief that David never knew when he was going to have his evenings free! 'I could give him a ring lunchtime, if you like,' she went on doubtfully, intending to do no such thing.

'No, I don't like. The invitation was for you, Lucy. I draw the line at taking David Asher along. If you're going to become a respectable married lady, it will be the last time I get the chance to wine and dine you,' Joe went on deliberately, and his words brought an angry flush to Lucy's cheeks.

'That was uncalled for!' she hissed, and he raised a brow, his smile mocking her.

'Was it? I don't think so. You belonged to me before ever you belonged to young Asher. You're mine—you always will be,' he stated, and Lucy gasped.

'How dare you? I won't stay here a moment longer and listen to—to——'

'To what? A reminder from the past you so desperately want to forget? Don't worry, I'm not going to entertain Asher with details of our former relationship, Let's call a truce and dine together—for old time's sake?'

His smile was still mocking, but she thought now it was self-mockery, and she couldn't resist him. He looked so—so *lost* somehow, so alone, but she managed to keep her voice cool and impersonal and hoped he would never know the effort it cost her. 'Yes, a dinner for old time's sake,' she agreed quietly. 'Tonight would be fine,' she hurried on, afraid that if it was left any longer she would back out.

'Tonight would be fine,' Joe echoed her words. 'Do you want me to pick you up at your home? Or shall we meet in town? You'd probably prefer that,' he added wryly, but Lucy shook her head.

'No, I should not! I'll be at home, Professor.' With a tilt of her proud head, she swept out, leaving Joe to smile ruefully to himself.

'You're going out with Joe?' Sadie looked stunned, and Lucy almost wished she had taken up Joe's suggestion of meeting in town, but it was too late now. Anyway, why should they have to hide away from her prying family?'

'Yes—he's going away and——' Lucy began to explain, but was given no opportunity to do so.

Sadie's face was a picture. 'Going away? For good?' She looked so sorrowful that a spurt of anger at Joe overcame Lucy for a moment.

'Oh, Sadie, pet! Don't lose your heart to him! Anyway, all he's doing is taking me out to dinner. It isn't a romantic evening with soft lights and a thousand violins playing,' Lucy pointed out, beginning to brush her hair into some sort of style.

'Where's he going to?' Sadie demanded, her face mutinous.

Lucy hesitated. 'He's due a few days' holiday. I don't really know *where* he's going. He's got relatives somewhere. I dare say,' she said vaguely, giving up the attempt at sorting out her wayward hair. 'I think I'll leave it loose,' she said to no one in particular, but that didn't suit Sadie, either.

'Oh, yes, you do that, Lucy Powell! You just do that!' Sadie flung at her, and Lucy whirled around. 'Leave it loose so—so Joe can run his fingers through it and—and——' Sadie's convoluted sentence was broken off by a sob, and she rushed from the bedroom. Lucy heard the bathroom door slam, and she sank wearily on to the bed, her hairbrush dangling from her unsteady hand.

If she had had lovesickness all those years ago, it was nothing to what Sadie was suffering. How could Joe, how *could* he? The thought of Joe teasing Sadie's luxuriant black hair around his finger almost choked her, and she hurled the brush across the room, wishing he could feel its force. Of all the low-down, conniving scoundrels! She clenched her fists, then glared at the bedroom door, wishing Joe was within reach. Well, she would tell him a few home truths tonight—their last social engagement together would be one to remember, she could promise him that!

If Joe noticed the high spots of angry colour in her cheeks later that evening, he didn't comment on it. Instead he turned his sensuous smile upon Sadie and on Lucy's father, her mother having departed for home as suddenly as she had arrived.

Sadie seemed to be over her hurt and anger, fortunately, and hung on Joe's every word. 'I hear you're off on holiday, Joe. Where to?' she asked bluntly, and he looked startled for a moment.

'Back up north, where my roots are, pet,' he said easily, and Lucy flinched at the simple endearment. 'I thought I'd look up a few old friends, then decide what's to be done about my cottage,' he went on.

'Oh? You aren't selling up, are you?' Sadie asked suspiciously, but Joe's evasive smile told them nothing, and before her father had a chance to ask Joe any personal questions Lucy was ready and being whisked away. It seemed that Joe was eager to get away as well.

'You're quiet, Lucy. Yet I sense that your little brain's seething away with messages,' Joe commented as they travelled at least a mile without Lucy venturing to speak. She couldn't; she was too full.

'My brain's always seething,' she said sweetly, then deliberately lay back against the seat and closed her eyes. Later she would tell him what she thought of him, but now wasn't the time.

The restaurant was one of her own favourites, not far from the theatre and, like the theatre, it overlooked the calm waters of the Avon. Their table was set out on the terrace, and Lucy caught her breath at the magic in the air—the warm summer evening, silver gleaming in the light from pink-shaded wall-lights, a single rose in a slender glass vase on their table, the sunlit waters of the river, and, best of all, the man she loved smiling at her across the table. If only that love could flare anew!

She was hardly aware that she sighed, but Joe's gaze sharpened. 'Something not to your liking, little Lucy?' he asked gently, then dropped his gaze to the menu as if her answer did not interest him.

'No, everything's fine, thank you, Joe. There's a lovely view of the theatre from here,' she went on, striving to be pleasant, at least for the time being. What use was revenge, anyway? She couldn't bring

back the past, couldn't prevent Sadie from falling into
the same trap from which she herself was only now
escaping. She would have this one evening to look back
on.

'I would have booked theatre tickets, but that's
something you need to do well in advance. Anyway,
Shakespeare's old hat to you, isn't he?' His eyes smiled
into hers, but now there was a subtle difference. His
gaze was frankly admiring, and Lucy was glad she had
taken such pains with her appearance. This time she
wasn't wearing anything of Sadie's, not even the gold
chains. Her dress was new, bought in a few minutes
snatched from her nursing duties. The rich glowing
emerald was the perfect foil for her bright hair, which
she left unconfined for once, and the knowledge that
she was looking her best did wonders for her self-
esteem. She positively glowed, and as she glanced out
at the river the crystal earrings in her neat little ears
sparkled in the light.

'Pretty earrings. A gift from the lucky man?' Joe
asked, and she agreed that they were. In actual fact,
she had bought them at lunchtime in Stratford, feeling
they were just what she needed to go with the dress.

Pleasant small talk punctuated the meal, and Joe
made everything easy, not touching on personal matters or on controversial subjects. They were just finishing the salmon poached in champagne when the first
note of discord sounded. 'Did you tell Sadie I was
going away?' Joe asked, and, stonily, Lucy nodded.

'Yes; was that wrong of me?'

'The temperature's dropped several degrees out
here,' Joe commented, his eyes gleaming. 'Did I say
something I shouldn't have done?'

'Sadie's a lovely girl, kind and—and generous!' Lucy burst out. 'She's very upset about you going away, but I told her it was only for a few days.'

'Perhaps you should give her my address up north. I'll let you have it,' Joe said easily, and Lucy hastily glanced down at her plate, attempting to hide the anguish in her eyes.

'Why don't you invite her out to dinner before you go?' she suggested recklessly. 'She was rather put out because you're treating *me* tonight.'

'She'll get over it.' Joe's tone was careless, and Lucy froze.

'Like I did, I suppose? Yes, I dare say she will,' she agreed. 'How is Rosemary, by the way?' Deliberately she introduced the former Mrs Joe Kingsley into the conversation, and Joe winced.

'She's doing very well, thank you,' he said, after a moment. 'I think she'll find the advantages of the operation outweigh the disadvantages.' He paused, then went on slowly, 'She's several years older than me, Lucy, and we spent our married life in a desperate attempt to find out why we couldn't have a child. At least *she* was desperate,' he amended, meeting Lucy's gaze frankly. 'I like children, certainly, but they aren't essential for married bliss. Companionship, shared interests; these things count more the older you get.'

Lucy was silent for a moment. 'I didn't know—I thought you were happily married when we had our relationship.' Reluctantly she forced out the words, and Joe made a small sound—of pain, perhaps; she couldn't be sure.

'I don't go around seducing young virgins, if that's what you think of me,' he said shortly, then hesitated, choosing his words carefully. 'At the time, Rosemary and I were going through a bad patch in our marriage. We weren't even living together, despite what the hospital gossips might have suggested.' His voice hardened. 'Neither of us wanted a divorce, but that's what it came to. We got divorced while I was working in London. What happened between you and me, Lucy, was inevitable, but——'

Lucy's gaze was intent. 'Please—don't! I understand. You were lonely and frustrated, and I was only too willing. It's over now.' She dismissed their love-affair as if it had meant as little to her as it obviously had to Joe. 'Anyway, history seems to be repeating itself, doesn't it? It's Sadie who's of more interest to me at the moment. She's fallen violently in love with you, but you don't seem to care! She can't see that you're too old and too experienced for her!'

'Nor could you all that time ago,' Joe pointed out coolly. 'I'm sorry she's suffering from unrequited love, but she'll get over it. *I* certainly haven't given her any reason to suppose I've taken a fancy to her. And love doesn't enter into it,' he finished bitterly.

Lucy tossed back her hair, her gaze mutinous, and Joe laughed softly. 'You look absolutely irresistible when you're burning with anger, Lucy, love! So irresistible that I'm sorry I'm not young any more. I hope Asher knows the prize of gold he's getting. I doubt that he does.'

Before a startled Lucy could think of something crushing to say, Joe changed the subject. He seemed determined to keep the conversation on medical matters, and expounded at some length his thoughts on the running of the home-care scheme so far.

'I think we've solved the main difficulties. The community nurses are beginning to see that the scheme *will* work, and that we're not taking away all the easier-to-manage patients. I hope we can look forward to a full integration of services before long. Now, I've got a few ideas and I'd like your opinion.'

Joe's voice had warmed as it always did when he was talking about patients, and Lucy was so carried away by his enthusiasm that she quite forgot how angry she was, and they were just finishing their second coffee before she realised how late it was getting.

'Time you were tucked up in bed, Lucy.' Joe's smile was indulgent, tender, and, though Lucy suspected she was being treated like a favourite niece rather than an attractive and eligible woman, she didn't bridle as she might have done earlier in the evening. The food, good wine and coffee had relaxed her; so had the conversation, which Joe kept flowing easily. His manner was relaxed, too, as if he had set out to make her enjoy herself and had enjoyed himself as a bonus, surprising himself as well as her.

Not another word was said about Sadie, and when Joe suggested a stroll by the river Lucy agreed. He kept his arm lightly about her shoulders as they walked, and, although his touch was bitter-sweet, she made no attempt to shrug him off. For once she was at peace, and the beautiful velvety evening was everything it should have been. All they needed, she felt, was a thousand violins playing the love theme from *Doctor Zhivago*!

All they needed, too, was words of love between them, but that could never be. If only there wasn't Harry Hamilton! Sadie she now dismissed from her

mind. Joe was probably just being kind to the girl, and
Sadie, like the younger Lucy, had read too much into
his interest. But there was no doubt that his ex-wife
still loomed large in his life, despite their obviously
unhappy marriage. For Lucy herself there was no
room. A sigh broke from her, and Joe stopped.

'Cold, Lucy?' Joe's voice was tender, concerned, and
numbly Lucy shook her head.

'No, I'm not cold. Just—just tired,' she went on
quickly. Just suffering from a broken heart, but it isn't
fatal, Professor Kingsley, she said silently. Then Joe's
lips brushed lightly across her brow, and unthinkingly
she pulled his head down and pressed her mouth to
his. Joe's strong arms tightened about her, moulding
her to his body, and a tremor shot through her. She
felt his lips gently kiss her eyelids, then his mouth
drifted down to her throat, and she moved ecstatically
as his lips left a fiery trail on their way to the soft swell
of her breasts. Her legs threatened to give way under
her as Joe's exploring hands followed his lips. Then his
mouth found hers again, his tongue blazing new trails,
finding new ways to excite and arouse her, and Lucy
lost all track of time.

Then they broke apart, Joe's harsh breathing matching her own. After a long moment, he said, 'I'm not
going to apologise, Lucy. I've been wanting to kiss you
properly ever since our paths crossed again.'

His voice was harsh, troubled, and Lucy started to
tell him that it didn't matter, that she understood that
it was the magical evening, the moonlight and too
much wine, but she wasn't given the chance, for he
enfolded her in his arms once more and kissed her until
her head spun. No doubt some of it was the wine, but

she liked to believe it was also love, *her* love, over-powering them both and causing both their hearts to beat as one.

At long last he released her, and, shaken, Lucy managed the glimmer of a smile. 'Too much wine and moonlight,' she said brokenly.

Joe brushed back a lock of hair. 'Yes, that's what it was, Lucy. I'm sorry—I rather forgot we were celebrating your engagement to another man! Come on, we'd better get you home.'

He took her hand, squeezed it briefly, then hurried her along back the way they had come, leaving her no time to protest, tell him that she wasn't engaged to another man. But, no, she wouldn't tell him. All the while he believed she was marrying David Asher, he wouldn't realise how her heart ached for him. Joe genuinely cared for her, and he wanted her, now, this very moment. But it wasn't love, and another affair with him would solve nothing.

Only one light was burning in her father's cottage when they got back after a silent drive, and Joe refused Lucy's offer of coffee.

'But you must, Joe!' Surprising herself, Lucy begged him to stay. 'You haven't drunk nearly as much as I have, but you need to sleep it off, and you can't drive along that cart-track in the dark!'

'No, I'll go back to my flat in the hospital,' he assured her, 'but thank you for taking care of me, little Lucy.' Gently his lips touched hers. 'Goodnight, sleep tight!'

'Thank you for the meal and—and for everything,' she whispered. 'Goodnight, Joe.'

Goodnight, my love, she said silently as he drove

away, then turned, startled, at a sound from within. The door swung back and Sadie stood there, a reproachful expression on her round face. 'Enjoyed yourself, our Lucy?'

'Mm, it was lovely. I thought about you when we were eating,' Lucy said quickly. 'Salmon poached in champagne! How about that, then? It's just the sort of dish you would have enjoyed cooking, never mind eating. I'm that tired, I could fall into bed. Is Dad all right?' she went on, since Sadie still stood there, staring at her rather dolefully.

'Dad? Oh, aye, he's champion. He went to bed early. I think he's missing Mam,' Sadie said quickly, and Lucy nodded, her eyes sympathetic.

'I expect you are, too, aren't you? She—you and Mum are much closer than she and I ever were. Well, I'm off to roost—did you bolt up at the back?'

Sadie seemed to rouse herself. 'Yes, everything's done. You know, I've been thinking. I think I'll go back up home, just for a bit. I can always come back again. I might like to live down here permanently—it all depends, doesn't it?' With a brilliant smile, which failed to disguise the tears in her eyes, Sadie darted upstairs, leaving Lucy to gaze after her, perplexed.

'Oh, by the way, Lucy——' Sadie turned when she was on the half-landing '—did Joe say when he's going up? He could give me a lift, couldn't he? I'll ask him tomorrow.' She disappeared around the corner of the stairs, leaving Lucy rooted to the spot, but no longer perplexed.

CHAPTER ELEVEN

'OH, LUCY, will you tell Joe I can't see him tonight?'

Dr Harry's voice broke into Lucy's thoughts, and she glanced up, surprise holding her silent for a moment. 'But he's away! I thought he'd gone back up north. Should we expect him in today, then?'

Harry shook her head. 'No, I don't believe so. As far as I know, he's at his home, honey. Why? Did he say he was going away?' Harry's brows puckered in a frown, and Lucy patted her shoulder. Just lately Harry had been doing a lot of frowning and clearly was a very unhappy woman. Joe again!

'He told me he was going up north, just to see to his cottage up there and visit a few friends.'

'Ah, that'll be because he's selling up! His career's down here now, he told me. He certainly hasn't gone yet; I was talking to him on the phone just this morning,' Harry went on. 'You've got his home number, haven't you? Just call him for me—he'll understand.' She slung her tote bag across her shoulder, then waved. 'See you tomorrow!'

Lucy gazed after the doctor in astonishment, then, her mind whirling, she dialled Joe's private number, her fingers not quite steady. So, Joe hadn't gone up north, after all, but Sadie had! She'd been gone two days now, yet she must have known that Joe had changed his mind, since she had been confident of a lift.

It made no sense. Nor did Joe's cheerful acceptance of Harry's message. 'Is Harry tied up, then? Pity, but never mind. She wanted to see the pool I'm making,' Joe went on. 'Would you like to see my goldfish pool, Lucy? Bring young Asher along, if you like,' he went on quickly, and Lucy stifled a sigh. Most certainly she wasn't taking young Asher along!

'He's rather tied up at present. Ivor—Mr Browne—he's found David some extra——'

'Ah, good old Ivor! Did he speak to you, by the way?' Joe still sounded cheerful, and Lucy began to hate him for it.

'What about? I've hardly seen him all day. He seems remarkably perky,' Lucy went on, 'and so do you. Is there something I ought to know?' she went on brightly, yet dreading the answer. She was in no mood to congratulate him on his engagement to Harry, if indeed that was in the offing.

There was silence for a moment, then came Joe's husky chuckle. 'No, should there be? I was just thinking of all the pleasure my goldfish pond will give me in years to come,' he added, and Lucy giggled.

'Oh, Joe! I can't see you sitting in the twilight of your years gazing enraptured at *fish*!'

'That's better. A smile a day keeps the surgeon away, you know,' Joe went on, sounding satisfied. 'Did Harry tell you? She's going back home for Thanksgiving, and we're getting a replacement—a handsome Swede this time, would you believe?'

'I didn't know Harry was going home! She never said. Anyway, Thanksgiving isn't until November, is it?'

'That's right. I was over there for one and I wouldn't

have missed it for the world. How about the two of us having our own Thanksgiving here? It's a lovely afternoon; we could have tea on the lawn.'

'Perhaps I should bring a chaperon,' Lucy said softly, hating herself for destroying the spell Joe was beginning to cast, but knowing the foolishness of spending the evening alone at his cottage.

'Yes, perhaps you should,' he agreed heavily. 'Come anyway. Bring Sadie if you want—or your father,' he suggested. 'We could——'

'But she's gone!' Lucy interrupted. 'Sadie—she's gone back up north! She said she was going to ask you for a lift—she thought *you* were going home,' she added.

'Ah! She must have changed her mind about asking me, then. Is she going back for good? Well?' Joe went on testily when Lucy hestitated, and she glared at the receiver.

'She followed you, Joe. Or thought she had. I'm sure she never had the idea of going home before; she likes it down here. You must have encouraged her to—to think that you were interested!' she charged.

'This conversation is getting us nowhere, Lucy, and think of the unit's telephone bill,' Joe said evasively, and Lucy nodded to herself. He didn't need to say any more. What he *didn't* say was so obvious.

'I'd better go, then,' she said evenly. 'I've still got two patients to see, then I promised to——' She hesitated, wondering if Joe would feel she was overstepping the mark, but he prompted her to go on. 'I said I'd speak to a group of district nurses. Five of them, actually. They're the twilight nurses and I wanted to set their minds at rest. They've got a few

questions about the scheme that no one seems inclined
to answer, so I told Mr Browne I'd do it—is that all
right?' she rushed on.

'What if I say it isn't?'

Lucy floundered, then plunged on bravely. 'I don't
care! I'm going to speak to them anyway!'

'Good for you, little Lucy! Show 'em what you're
made of!' Joe approved. 'See you later!'

Lucy was left holding the receiver, listening to the
whirling noise after Joe put down the receiver at his
end. Joe Kingsley was as changeable as the weather.

It was early evening before Lucy found her way to
Joe's house, and it was only with reluctance that she
had made the decision to visit him. If it hadn't been for
Mr Browne's cautious words of praise, she told herself,
she certainly wouldn't have taken the risk, but praise
from Ivor Browne! It was unheard of, and she found
herself eager to tell Joe about it.

Joe greeted her without surprise. 'Glad you could
tear yourself away from those twilight nurses, Lucy!
Come in, make yourself at home,' he invited, and Lucy
wished desperately she could.

'I'll put the kettle on.' Joe's voice floated out to her
from the kitchen, his long legs having carried him to
the rear of the house before she had ventured across
the threshold. From the state of the hall, he had clearly
been doing some decorating, and Lucy stepped gingerly
over a bucket of paste and several rolls of wallpaper.

'I'm glad you're keeping busy—are you buying the
house, after all?' she asked as she entered the bright
kitchen, her gaze softening at sight of Joe in a domestic
setting, a flowered apron tied around his waist.

'Yes, my offer's been accepted. I shouldn't alter anything until the purchase goes through, but the DIY urge overcame me! I'm not terribly domesticated, though, so you'll have to wash up afterwards. I can just about make myself a cup of tea,' he added, opening a wall cupboard and bringing down various tins. 'Ginger biscuits in there—oh, and flapjacks in this one.' He pointed to the brightly coloured canisters. 'Help yourself.'

Lucy selected a flapjack and nibbled it daintily while Joe set out the mugs. 'Tea's masting. Won't be a minute,' he murmured, then straddled the kitchen chair, his long legs almost touching hers as she sat on a high stool at the breakfast bar. She forced her eyes down to the flapjack, every nerve on edge. Joe was looking delightfully casual in an open-necked shirt and rather scruffy jeans. He hadn't shaved, either, and the dark bristles gave him a buccaneer appearance that was very sensuous. He was difficult to resist at the best of times, but dressed like that he was irresistible. He looked younger than his years, too, like an overgrown schoolboy. Lucy had the urge to smooth back that lock of recalcitrant hair that kept falling over his left eye, to sew on the button that was half hanging off his shirt, to snatch off the apron and tell him he shouldn't have to fend for himself.

But she could do none of these things, so she launched into her carefully prepared speech. 'Mr Browne called me in this afternoon,' she began, unable to keep the triumph out of her voice.

Joe raised a brow, dark eyes glinting with laughter. 'And?' he prompted.

'I was a bit flustered, as you can well imagine,' Lucy

went on, a little smile playing about the corners of her mouth. 'I went over all the misdemeanours I might have committed, but I couldn't think I'd done anything *that* awful, and do you know? He wanted to congratulate me on my good work!'

Joe laughed at the expression on her face. 'Don't sound so amazed, Lucy. Even Ivor knows a good nurse when he sees one! He's pleased with the way the home-care scheme is going now, and so am I—particularly pleased with my liaison nurse, Miss Powell,' he added gently, and Lucy flushed with pleasure.

'Why, thank you, Professor, dear,' she said, casting her eyes down modestly, drawing another laugh from Joe. If only they could always be like this. 'Mr Browne said I'd done very well and I wasn't too young after all! It must have cost him something to admit that—he was the one who said I was too young to be a ward sister,' Lucy went on, and Joe nodded, clearly enjoying her surprise.

'You still look about seventeen, Staff Nurse, but we'll make a ward sister of you yet, so don't worry— but perhaps you're not so ambitious now?' he suggested easily.

'Why shouldn't I be? I still think I could run a ward, though I must admit I'd rather be doing basic nursing. I miss bedside nursing,' she went on reflectively.

'It isn't absolutely settled yet, but I think we can count on having enough funds for the scheme for at least another year. We'll have to see how things work out,' Joe told her, his eyes on her face, but Lucy's mind was already busy with what she had to tell him, knowing he wouldn't like it.

'Does that mean my job's safe for another year?'

'If you want it?' There was a question mark at the end of Joe's statement, and Lucy glanced down at her hands. Then he startled her by clasping her small hands in his own, and she hoped he wouldn't feel the acceleration in her pulse-rate.

'I don't think I do.' With an effort, she raised her eyes, expecting to see anger or condemnation in his, but finding neither. 'I think I ought to return to ward nursing. I've enjoyed being liaison nurse, really I have, Joe,' she hastened to reassure him, 'but perhaps I'm not cut out for—for this sort of work. It's back to the TPR rounds and dressings for me!' she finished, relieved that she had got it off her chest.

'If that's what you want, then I'm sure you're right to make the break,' Joe agreed quietly. 'You'll have to finish your contract, but I've no objection to your going for interviews whenever you like. I suppose you'll want to leave the hospital altogether?'

Lucy's eyes mirrored her indecision. 'Perhaps,' she said. But then she would be miles away from Joe. If she returned to the main wards at the hospital, she would at least see him sometimes. Surely that was better than not seeing him at all, no matter that he might be married to Harry—or back with Rosemary. . . 'How is your ex-wife now? Is she still getting on well?' Her mouth felt dry and it was more than she could do to form the name 'Rosemary', but Joe wouldn't know that.

He shrugged. 'I haven't seen her since yesterday, but she calls me every day. Once she's well again, I don't suppose I'll see much of her. We remain friends, Lucy. All the bitterness and recrimination is in the past now,' he added, releasing her hands abruptly.

'I'd better be getting back—unless you want to show me the lake you're digging?' Lucy suggested with a little smile.

'Come on, then. A quick peek, then I must finish the wall.' Without waiting for her, Joe went out on to the patio and Lucy followed more slowly.

'Will you be back on Monday? Or will you go up north for a while, after all?'

Joe indicated the small pool area, which Lucy could see was already completed. 'I'll have to rest it for a while, introduce plants and let them settle in before I can get any fish,' he told her. 'Yes, perhaps I might go up north later. I. . .' He shrugged, without finishing the sentence, then turned and smiled slowly to her. 'Why don't you come up with me? You could stay with your mother and visit me at my little hideaway! You might bring your father,' he suggested.

'Yes, that's an idea,' she agreed, intending to do nothing of the sort. Watching Sadie throw herself at Joe again wasn't something she cared to do; then there were her parents. . . 'Mum hasn't phoned again,' she went on slowly. 'I think both she and my father realise that there's nothing left between them, only memories. Sadie's happy with my mother and I'm happy with my father. We're meant to be two halves of a family rather than one complete,' Lucy went on, a trace of bitterness in her voice.

'Oh, Lucy, don't!' Joe's arms opened and Lucy ran into them. She felt sure she hadn't made the move, but she must have done. They stood, arms about each other, Lucy's head resting against Joe's chest, her eyes closed. If there was a heaven, then this was it. All her problems tumbled away from her as she raised her tear-stained face for his kiss. Whatever happened in the future, this was where she belonged. Never mind Sadie and Rosemary and Harry, and her parents. She needed no one but Joe, now or ever.

The kiss was brief, Lucy's heaven lasting no more than a few moments, but she was reluctant for the embrace to end. 'My little flower,' Joe crooned, stroking her soft hair and drawing a sigh of bliss from her. 'I could get addicted to you,' he went on, reluctantly releasing her, 'but this won't get the hall redecorated. Do you want to lend a hand? No, probably not,' he commented, glancing down at her pretty floral suit. It wasn't one of her workaday outfits and she had worn it specially for her visit.

'I'll stand over you and pretend I'm a nursing officer, shall I?' Lucy suggested, determined not to be a weeping willow and spoil their few moments of truce.

Joe's eyes twinkled at her. 'Why not?' He tucked her arm in his and they strolled back to the hall. It wasn't until he had picked up his wallpaper brush again that the truce was broken. 'Is Sadie staying up north for good? I thought she was settled down here now?' He turned back to the wall, evidently concentrating on what he was doing, but Lucy wasn't deceived.

'What gave you that idea? She was filling in time before she has to enter the job market—or become one of the unemployed,' Lucy said wearily. 'I haven't heard from her since she went home—I wonder if she's still looking for you?'

'I sincerely hope not, Lucy!' There was laughter in Joe's voice. 'Now—tell me what you think of the pattern? I wanted something that wouldn't need matching. Decorating isn't one of my strong points either,' he admitted, 'but I wanted to do something different, work with my hands, just let my tired brain take it easy for a few days.' His gaze was intent as it rested on Lucy's face. 'Why didn't you bring Asher with you? Is Ivor still keeping him busy?'

'I—there's no need. . . I——' Lucy stopped, unsure of what to tell him.

'Still keeping the engagement a secret?' Joe asked casually, his face averted.

'There wasn't an engagement,' said coolly, tired of prevaricating, and Joe swung round, his eyes veiled. 'It was David—he didn't listen to what I was saying when I told him we wouldn't be happy. He's got someone else, I believe,' she said painfully.

'Yes, I've seen him with the sister on Shakespeare, but I didn't realise it was serious. I'm afraid I don't go in the canteen much, nor do I listen to the grapevine,' he added meaningfully, and Lucy bit her lip, suddenly uncomfortable at his words.

'No, listening to it doesn't do anyone much good,' she agreed. 'Still, it once told me you were married, didn't it? I wasn't grateful to it then, but I am now,' she hurried on, suddenly resentful, and Joe shrugged, his back still to her.

'I hope we aren't going to quarrel, Lucy,' he said quietly.

'No, of course we aren't,' she agreed. 'There's no reason why we can't be friends now.'

'There's every reason!' Joe objected. 'We can never be friends, Lucy. Lovers, certainly; enemies, perhaps; but never friends.'

'You'd better get back up to Northumberland and make friends with Sadie, then!' she retorted.

She could have bitten out her tongue a moment later for Joe agreed that perhaps he should. 'At least Sadie isn't always listing my faults!' he added bitterly, and Lucy gasped.

'I didn't know you had any faults, Joe Kingsley!' she flared, hands on hips.

'I might have one or two,' he admitted, a glimmer of a smile in his voice. 'Sadie never told me that, though. She probably thinks the run rises at my bidding every morning,' he went on, beginning to whistle tunelessly as he reached for the wallpaper. 'One more wall, then I can knock off. Union supper break,' he added with an outrageous grin. 'Why don't you join me? We could talk about wor Sadie,' he went on, and Lucy nearly choked before seeing the funny side of it.

'You sound like my mother! It was "wor Sadie" this and "wor Sadie" that! Anyway, about Sadie——'

'If we weren't talking about Sadie, we could talk about Harry Hamilton,' Joe suggested easily, waving the brush about.

'If you aren't going to finish tonight, you'd better cover the paste up. It'll go hard,' Lucy told him firmly, and meekly he did as he was bid, then tried ineffectually to brush his clothes down. 'Yes, we could talk about Harry,' she agreed, resisting the urge to help him brush off the dried paste. 'I expect she'll come tomorrow,' she went on painfully, aware that Joe was watching her, an odd expression in his eyes.

'She'll probably wait until I've sorted out my private life—or "gotten your personal life into shape, Joe Kingsley", which is what she told me yesterday,' he added, a gleam in his eye.

'Oh—Rosemary,' Lucy said forlornly, and Joe

looked up, the button on his shirt having at last given
way.

'Damn! Are you any good at sewing, Lucy? No,
that's wor Sadie, isn't it? I forgot,' he went on,
defending himself with a raised arm as Lucy threw a
scrap of wallpaper at him. 'Where were we? Ah, yes;
Rosemary. Well,' he went on, wiping his hands on a
rag, 'she'll not want me once she's feeling better, and
Harry's taking a day off to see her ex again, though I
doubt that anything will come of it. I told her she had
to get her personal life into shape if I had to, and she
took me at my word,' Joe continued, wiping his brow
on his arm. 'It's getting warm, Lucy. Fetch us a
lemonade, there's a good girl.'

Lucy tugged her forelock and, smiling to herself, did
as she was asked. When she returned it was to find that
Joe had removed his shirt, and was standing with it in
his hand, tugging experimentally at the other buttons.
'Ah, lovely! While you're here you can sew them all on
for me. Just what I need, thank you,' he added, taking
the glass her suddenly shaky hand was holding out to
him.

'You'd better send for Sadie,' she said tartly, taking
her own glass off the tray and perching on the bottom
stair. She surveyed Joe over the rim of the glass as she
drank. He wasn't a hairy man but she knew from
experience that he had a few dark hairs running down
from his chest to his—— Hastily, she put down her
glass and got up, brushing an imaginary speck off her
pretty skirt.

'I ought to be getting along now, Joe. I hate to
interrupt your painting and decorating business! Do

you want more?' She held out the jug of lemonade invitingly, and a slow grin spread across Joe's face.

'More what, little Lucy?' he asked innocently, and she coloured, the more so because she couldn't deny the trend of her throughts, and hoped fervently he hadn't read her mind!

'Lemonade, Professor Kingsley.' Her voice was sharp but Joe didn't take offence at it, merely holding out his glass for her to pour.

'Thank you, Staff Nurse Powell,' he said, matching her formality. 'Now, I think you had better go—oh, take my shirt with you, will you? And the buttons. I'll pick it up on Monday.' He raised a brow as Lucy stifled a gasp. 'You don't mind, do you?' he asked in apparent surprise.

Lucy's lips twitched. 'No, of course not, sir. Only too happy to oblige!'

'You could parcel it up and send it to Sadie, if you really *can't* sew on buttons,' he suggested. 'Or Rosemary might do it for me when she's feeling better,' he went on remorselessly, setting down his glass and eyeing her. 'Then there's Harry—now *she's* handy with a needle. She——'

'Oh—oh, you!' Lucy exploded, then, unable to keep a straight face, she dissolved into laughter. 'You're arrogant and chauvinistic, that's what you are, Joe Kingsley!' she went on, still spluttering with laughter. 'You——' Tears became mixed in with the laughter, like a light shower of rain falling while the sun was shining, and she hastily picked up the tray and took it into the kitchen, glad that Joe hadn't seen the tears.

Joe made no attempt to follow her into the kitchen, and when at length Lucy returned to the hall, her mind was made up. 'I've been thinking,' she began, and Joe raised a brow. He was leaning against the paste-table, arms folded across his bare chest, a frown on his face.

'So have I, but you first,' he said, unsmiling.

'I thought about your taking us up to the north. That would be lovely. My father would enjoy the trip and— and we might bring Sadie back with us,' Lucy offered. 'I don't think she intended staying up there long,' she hurried on. 'You and she could—could get to know each other better.'

Joe's eyes narrowed. 'I already know Sadie better than I ever intended,' he said wryly.

'Oh! You and Sadie—you have a nerve, Joe Kingsley!' Lucy shot at him. Never had she dreamed that Joe and Sadie were lovers! 'You—no, you wouldn't,' she acknowledged.

'Can I join in the conversation now?' he asked softly, coming towards her. 'No, I wouldn't make love to Sadie. I took her to the theatre partly because she dropped so many damn hints, and partly because I hoped an evening with me would cure her infatuation. It didn't,' he said flatly. 'She's a lovely child, warm and friendly, but she *is* just that—a child. I'm old enough to be her father—it's a wonder she didn't tell you I made her mad because I told her to grow up first, *then* come back to see if I'm as irresistible as she thought. Rather like the case of a certain Student Nurse Lucinda Powell, I should think,' he went on slowly, and Lucy nodded.

'Yes, it was.' Her voice was low. 'I threw myself at you, didn't I? Not that you made any move to evade me!' she flung at him, and he gravely acknowledged that.

'I couldn't resist you, Lucy. That's all there was to it,' he said simply, then shrugged aside his youthful ardour. 'Your pert little face burned a hole in my conscience for a long time afterwards, if that's any consolation. But I thought—I suppose I thought you would get over it, find some other hero to worship.'

'I never did. It was only you, Joe.' It was Lucy's turn to shrug, her gesture saying eloquently enough that the past was over. 'Anyway, that's all over now. If you genuinely care for Sadie——'

Angrily he brushed her words aside. 'If you genuinely care for David Asher, you——'

'But I don't! I—I don't care for anyone now!' she assured him, swiftly.

'Good!' That makes two of us, doesn't it? That way neither of us will make the same mistake again. Why don't you stay the night, little Lucy? We both want each other. If there's no love involved, so much the better,' he went on conversationally, and Lucy stared at him, thunderstruck. 'I need you, Lucy. Sadie will keep for later—perhaps next year, when she's grown up a little,' he added savagely, and Lucy launched herself at him, pummelling at his chest with her little fists.

'I hate you, Joe Kingsley and—and Sadie's more than welcome to you!' she flung at him, her spurt of anger dying as rapidly as it had erupted as Joe's hands crept to her face, and his lips descended on hers.

'Do you still think I want Sadie?' he asked after a long moment, one hand reaching out to stroke her hair while the other remained firmly about her waist.

'No, perhaps not,' Lucy agreed wanly. 'Perhaps it's me you want *now*, but——'

'Perhaps it's you I *love* now, little Lucy,' he amended, and she raised her startled blue eyes to his. 'I'm too old for you, pet, and it could be that Rosemary's childlessness can be laid at *my* door,' he went on painfully, wanting to be sure that Lucy understood. 'The tests suggested there was no reason why I couldn't father a child, but there was no reason for Rosemary's barrenness, either. It was just one of those things. If having children is important for you. . .' Joe waited, his nerves taut.

'I belong to you—and you belong to me,' Lucy said simply, doing her bit for Women's Lib by standing on tiptoe and kissing him full on the mouth.

Joe chuckled. 'You need longer legs, wor Lucy! Here, I'll give you a hand.' He swept her up in his arms so that her face was on a level with his. 'Is that better, hinny?' he asked softly, a glow in his eyes that Lucy couldn't mistake.

'Well, it might be,' she murmured, then laughter overcame her, to be followed by a swift tide of passion as their lips met again, all thoughts of decorating the hall going completely out of their minds!

4 MEDICAL ROMANCES
AND 2 FREE GIFTS
From Mills & Boon

Capture all the excitement, intrigue and emotion of the busy medical world by accepting four FREE Medical Romances, plus a FREE cuddly teddy and special mystery gift. Then if you choose, go on to enjoy 4 more exciting Medical Romances every month! Send the coupon below at once to:

> **MILLS & BOON READER SERVICE, FREEPOST**
> **PO BOX 236, CROYDON, SURREY CR9 9EL.**
> No stamp required

- ✂ - ✂→

YES! Please rush me my 4 Free Medical Romances and 2 Free Gifts! Please also reserve me a Reader Service Subscription. If I decide to subscribe, I can look forward to receiving 4 Medical Romances every month for just £5.80 delivered direct to my door. Post and packing is free, and there's a free Mills & Boon Newsletter. If I choose not to subscribe I shall write to you within 10 days – I can keep the books and gifts whatever I decide. I can cancel or suspend my subscription at any time. I am over 18.

EP02D

Name (Mr/Mrs/Ms) _____

Address _____

_____

_____ Postcode _____

Signature _____

The right is reserved to refuse an application and change the terms of this offer. Offer expires **July 31st 1991**. Readers in Southern Africa write to P.O.Box 2125, Randburg, South Africa. Other Overseas and Eire, send for details. You may be mailed with other offers from Mills & Boon and other reputable companies as a result of this application. If you would prefer not to share in this opportunity, please tick box. ☐

Mills & Boon

— *MEDICAL* ♥ *ROMANCE* —

The books for your enjoyment this month are:

GOODBYE TO YESTERDAY Sarah Franklin
CALLING NURSE HILLIER Elizabeth Petty
LUCY'S CHALLENGE Hazel Fisher
NO LEASE ON LOVE Jean Evans

♥   ♥   ♥   ♥   ♥

Treats in store!

Watch next month for the following absorbing stories:

ALWAYS ON MY MIND Laura Macdonald
TANSY'S CHILDREN Alice Grey
A BITTER JUDGEMENT Marion Lennox
HAWAIIAN HEALING Sara Burton

Available from Boots, Martins, John Menzies, W.H. Smith, Woolworths and other paperback stockists.

Also available from Mills and Boon Reader Service, P.O. Box 236, Thornton Road, Croydon, Surrey CR9 3RU.

Readers in South Africa — write to:
Independent Book Services Pty, Postbag X3010, Randburg, 2125, S. Africa.